AN INVITATION TO MURDER

A MARY BLAKE MYSTERY

A.G. BARNETT

ODDMOOR PRESS

MAILING LIST

G et FREE SHORT STORY *A Rather Inconvenient Corpse* by signing up to the mailing list at agbarnett.com

CHAPTER ONE

The insistent buzzing of the intercom finally forced Mary Blake from the sofa. She had been prepared to ignore it, assuming it was either someone selling something or, more likely, the press. But the insistence of whoever was at the door made that impossible.

She moved across the room to the small video panel that was set in the wall by the front door to her apartment. On it she saw the short, stocky figure of Dot Tanner. She was standing on the front step of the building, her arms folded impatiently, peering at the camera in an accusatory manner. Mary sighed and pressed the buzzer to release the door. There was no use in hoping Dot would give up, she didn't know the meaning of the phrase. She unlocked her front door and headed back to the soft, leather sofa where she took a large swig of her gin and tonic.

"Bloody hell, Mary!" Dot said as she burst in the door. "What the hell's the matter with you?!"

Without waiting for a reply, Dot moved to the tall windows set into three corners of the large living room and began opening the curtains.

The apartment was just one of the many things Mary knew she was going to have to give up now. She had barely been able to cover the mortgage as it was, particularly given the regular contributions she had to make to the family home, she certainly couldn't afford them now.

"Hey Dot, how're things?" Mary said airily, waving her gin glass.

"How're things?!" Dot said in her best 'annoyed parent' voice. "Oh things are just great, bearing in mind my best friend sacked me and now refuses to return my calls."

"Oh, you're not sacked," Mary said with another wave of her hand.

"Oh, aren't I?" Dot said, pausing with the final curtain only half opened. She turned to Mary with her hands on her hips, one eyebrow raised.

Dot Tanner was a stocky, middle-aged woman with mousy brown hair and delicate features set above a square jaw. She was in fact an almost complete counterpoint to Mary who was taller and with a heart shaped face, framed by her shoulder length dark hair.

"Come on, Dot, things said in the heat of the moment and all that."

"Well, it doesn't really matter if I'm sacked or not because there's no bloody work to do with you sitting on your rear end all day," Dot grumbled as she opened the final curtain.

"What else do you want me to do? I'm unemployed!"

"You're only unemployed because you won't answer your bloody phone, Terry's been trying to get hold of you."

"All Terry wants is to get me into commercials for old people," Mary said bitterly. "Bloody stair lifts and incontinence pants!"

Her agent, Terry Hope, like most of the TV world, had decided that her career was over which meant pitching her for adverts for increasingly embarrassing products and no real work to speak of.

"Nothing wrong with doing an advert or two to tide you over," Dot said as she began clearing the various chocolate bar wrappers from the coffee table in front of Mary. "It keeps your name out there and in people's minds. Anyway, it's got to be better than sitting in this pit, drinking gin and eating chocolate."

Mary ignored the reference to her rather expensive, and soon to be lost, London apartment as a "pit", and instead decided to focus on the more obvious mistake.

"To be honest, I can't think of anything better than laying around drinking gin and eating chocolate."

"Daytime drinking, though!" Dot said shaking her head.

"When would you prefer me to drink? When I'm asleep?"

Dot tutted and turned towards the kitchen, but stopped as her eye caught the TV screen.

"You're watching *The Morning Show*?" she said flatly.

"Yes," Mary said, hoping she didn't sound as guilty as she suddenly felt.

"So you've recorded it from this morning?"

"So what if I did?" Mary said defensively.

Dot gave her a look but said nothing. "What do you make of her then?" she said turning back to the screen.

"She hasn't been on yet," Mary answered, gaze fixed on the TV. She didn't want to meet Dot's eye right now.

She heard her friend move off into the kitchen and felt a pang of sadness in her chest. She knew she was behaving like a child, but she was hurting and she had no idea what she was going to do next. For twenty years she had played the role of Susan Law in the hit TV detective show, *Her Law* and now it was over. She had been let go and replaced in the lead role by a young, upcoming actress named Melanie Shaw.

Apparently, they had wanted to "freshen things up", but everyone knew what that meant. At fifty, she had reached the top of the hill and was now firmly heading down the other side. Apparently, women of a certain age weren't fit to be seen on prime time television taking down bad guys anymore. Maybe they were worried it would put people off their dinner, she thought bitterly.

The fact that Melanie Shaw would be taking over the role had felt like an additional blow. In her early twenties, with blonde hair, blue eyes and a smile that could turn anyone to butter, she seemed to signify everything that Mary suddenly felt she wasn't. Young, vibrant, drop dead gorgeous and trendy, whatever that was these days.

Right now, Mary felt like a has-been, and that wasn't like her. She had always been so confident, so assured of who she was and what she was doing. She was the sassy TV detective that the men wanted to marry and the women wanted to be.

Now though? Now she wasn't sure what she was.

She had found herself hating Melanie Shaw in the few short weeks since she had been told that she was being replaced. Oh, she knew it wasn't Melanie's fault, anyone would have jumped at the chance and she didn't even know the woman, but every time she thought of that face of flawless skin she wanted to punch it.

"Looking back, do you know when I should have realised it was the end of the road for me?" Mary asked as Dot reappeared with a cup of tea.

Dot sighed, "Go on then, if it helps you to go over it all again."

"It was when the papers started to refer to me as 'glamorous,'" Mary said as she swung her legs off of the sofa to face her friend sitting opposite her.

"Not sexy, beautiful, powerful, commanding. Just, glamorous."

"So? What's that got to do with anything?" Dot said sipping at her tea and taking one of the biscuits she had laid out on a plate on the table between them. "Glamorous is a compliment, isn't it?"

Mary shook her head at her friend. Dot was her best friend, but she really was useless when it came to understanding people. She was neat, orderly, and probably the best PA the world had ever seen. Which was lucky because Mary was about as organised as a bag of cats. What Dot Tanner was not, though, was a people person. That was firmly Mary's territory.

"Because, Dot," she said in an exasperated tone. "Glamorous is code for 'old'. It's the word they use for someone who's gone soggy around the edges."

"Oh, don't talk rubbish," Dot said dismissively. "You'll find a new role. And be back on your feet in no time. And if you're soggy around the edges then I must have been dunked a good few times in a hot tea."

"Oh, come on," Mary said, ignoring the self-deprecating compliment. "You're one of the few people on earth who knows my dirty secret, Dot. I can't bloody act! I could play Susan Law because she was basically me but with someone else's words. I got lucky. If I took another role, everyone would see through me."

"Or maybe you'd surprise yourself," Dot said, sipping at her tea with one eyebrow raised.

"Dot, you know I can't act! You were there when I tried to do that play, surely you can remember how bloody awful I was?"

"You just needed a bit more time, you're just a bit rusty after playing the same role for so long."

Mary noticed how her friend's eyes had darted away as she was saying this. She didn't believe a word of it any more than Mary did, but she was being a good friend.

"Anyway," Mary said, "you're not an over-dunked biscuit, you just need to make more of your natural assets, dress a bit sexier."

Dot peered at her as though she had just suggested she grew wings.

Mary fell back on the sofa again. "Playing Susan Law was the only thing I've ever done with my life that was any good, Dot."

"Oh, don't be so melodramatic," Dot chided.

"I'm serious Dot. The life I knew is over, now I'm just some layabout sucking up oxygen that some useful person could be using."

"What's this?" Dot asked, ignoring her. She leaned forward and picked up an envelope from the coffee table.

"Oh," Mary said, rolling her eyes. "An invitation from Pea to go to some idiotic party he's throwing."

Mary's brother was a kind-hearted soul. Generous to a fault and undoubtedly fun, he somehow always managed to throw terrible parties. She'd lost count of the number times they had ended either in disaster, such as the time he accidentally set the curtains on fire with some candles he was using for mood lighting, or the time people had made their excuses and left early when the ancient plumbing on the old family home had thrown raw sewage up into the kitchen causing the whole house to reek.

It had been a while since Percy had thrown any parties though, he couldn't afford to these days. The family estate, or what was left of it, had been a one pit ever since their father had left the place saddled with debts. They had realised too late that his mind had already been in the grip of the dementia which now had him in a care home.

Mary knew well enough the financial problems at her old family home, she had sent Percy enough of her money over the years. That hadn't seemed an issue before, Mary always had money. The problem was, she spent it as though it was burning a hole in her bank account. She was now only too aware that saving was not her forte. Without the money from *Her Law* things were going to have to be very different.

In short, the invitation from her brother to a party had surprised her. She had even wondered fleetingly if the party had been partly for her benefit, to cheer her up. Percy, or Pea, as she had called him since their youth, was like that. Always the one trying to hold the family together. He had been the one to step up when their father's memory had begun fading, and now he was the one who visited him in the nursing home regularly. For all his puppy dog enthusiasm and often questionable judgement, he was, at heart a hard worker who took responsibility when needed.

These days, most of Pea's time was spent managing the family estate, or what was left of it. Between the endless emergency maintenance that Blancham Hall seemed to require just to stay standing and her father's nursing home fees, the family fund was vanishing faster than a gin and tonic did around Mary at the moment.

"Well, I think a party is just what you need," Dot said, pulling the invitation from the envelope.

"Bloody hell, Dot, there is such a thing as privacy you know."

"It says here," Dot continued obliviously. "That it's a murder mystery party,"

"And?"

"Well, you've got to go to that, I mean, they'll have all the parts set out and assigned. They probably won't be able to do it if you don't come." She paused and squinted at the sheet of card in her hand.

"Hold on a minute, it says you can bring a guest here!"

"So what?"

"Well, bearing in mind you fired me the other

day, I'd say you owe me one, don't you? Anyway, I've always wanted to see your family home."

Dot had asked her many times if she could see Blancham Hall, but Mary had always managed to find some excuse or other to cancel any visit. The truth was, Mary herself avoided it when she could these days. She found the nostalgia was always tinged with sadness now, despite her happy times there as a child. Seeing her dad's once sharp and funny mind deteriorate there had given the place a different feel.

Mary looked up into Dot's fierce blue eyes and knew that she was never going to get out of this.

"Oh, bloody hell," she moaned, flopping her head back onto the sofa. "I guarantee I will hate every moment."

"Oh you always say that, and then within half an hour you're swinging from a chandelier and singing some filthy song."

"I have never swung from a chandelier in my life, Dot Tanner, and you know it."

"Only because you can't reach the things. Now phone Terry and see what he wants."

Mary groaned again and took her phone from the coffee table and dialled her agent. "It's no wonder I fired you, who on earth would want to pay someone to be their mother twenty-four-seven," she said to Dot as the line rang.

"I'll go and make you a coffee," Dot said standing up and heading towards the kitchen, taking Mary's glass, which still had half a gin and tonic in it.

Mary was about to protest when her agent, Terry Hope, answered.

"Mary! Where have you been!"

"Mostly I've been at home not answering your calls. What do you want, Terry?"

"What do I want? I want to speak to my best client, that's what I want!"

"And what do you want to speak to me about?" Mary asked, getting annoyed.

"How to make you filthy rich of course, isn't that what we're all in it for?"

"In case it's escaped your attention Terry, I'm not 'in' anything anymore. I'm a has-been. An ex-actor."

"Nonsense! We just need to pivot your career and get you into a new area. Why don't we meet up tomorrow and we can go through some options?"

Mary had no idea what this meant, but she was sure she didn't want to find out. When Terry started using words like "pivot", it normally meant he was about to try and sign you up to smiling sweetly as you descended in a stair lift. She leaned forward and saw the invite on the table in front of her.

"I'm sorry Terry, but I'm away this weekend. Can you call me next week? You just keep everything bubbling along and I'll speak to you then." She hung up before he could say anything and turned her phone onto silent.

"So did he have good news?" Dot said returning with two coffees.

"He just told us to have a great time this weekend."

"Oh, how nice of him," Dot said, eyeing Mary as though she didn't believe a word.

Mary's eye flicked to the TV where the young, vibrant figure of Melanie Shaw had just bounced onto to the sofa next to the guests.

Dot took the remote and turned it off. "And it's not going to do you any good watching her talk about how great her new job is," she said, ever the teacher in the room.

"In that case," Mary sighed, "can I interest you in a gin and tonic?"

CHAPTER TWO

"It is not possible to need this many clothes for a single weekend," Dot said as she loaded the last of Mary's bags into the back of her car. Mary, of course, had said she couldn't possibly lift them herself as she had only just painted her nails and they needed to dry. Dot had then pointed out that she could very well have painted her nails earlier giving them time to dry which Mary had resolutely ignored.

"I was going to pack light, but I couldn't decide what I would want to wear when I was there, so I thought I'd better just pack a lot of options so that I didn't make us late."

"How thoughtful of you," Dot said, slamming the boot shut with rather more force than was necessary.

They climbed in and Dot pulled the car out into the mid-morning London traffic.

"So, who do you think will be there?" Dot asked.

"Oh, the usual crowd that hangs around with Pea, I'd imagine."

"Why do you call him that by the way? Is it just short for Percy?" Dot said.

"No, it's not 'P', it's 'Pea'. As in the vegetable. Silly sod got one stuck up his nose when he was a kid." Mary laughed.

"So, what did Pea say on the phone when you called him? Have I got a part in this murder mystery party?" Dot asked.

"You're going to play my maid," Mary answered with a smirk.

"Oh, that's great that is," Dot grumbled. Her east London accent becoming stronger, as it always did when she was annoyed. "So, who are you playing then? The Queen?"

Mary laughed. "Not quite, I'm playing Lady Gossover, whoever she is."

"So, do I even have a name? Or am I just servant number three or something?"

Mary opened the folder on her lap and flicked to the third page. "Your name is Esther."

"Just Esther? No surname?"

Mary closed the folder and leaned back in her seat. "I think only the nobility get surnames, Dot."

"Well I'm sure it will be a fun crowd knowing your brother. He's always one for a good time."

Mary frowned as she stared out of the window. Something had been playing on her mind. Pea had been deliberately vague when she had asked who else was coming and for some reason it made her suspicious.

"I'm honestly not sure who's coming, he just said it would be a good crowd."

She leaned back in her seat and closed her eyes, signalling to Dot that she didn't want to talk anymore.

All she really wanted was to be back on her sofa, wallowing in her own misery.

MARY WAS WOKEN by a punch in the arm from Dot.

"How on earth do you do that?" Dot asked irritably.

"Do what?"

"Close your eyes and fall asleep like that! Even when I'm exhausted it takes me ages."

"I don't know, just always been able to. Where are we?"

"Well I woke you for a reason, we're here." Dot pointed out of the window to her right.

Mary shifted herself upright and saw the familiar flat face of Blancham Hall flashing between the tall trees that lined the road.

"Oh, that was quick."

"It tends to be if you sleep through all of it," Dot said bitterly.

"Sorry. A good drive was it?"

"Alright actually, no traffic and at least you going to sleep let me listen to my gardening podcast. We're going to be early."

"Great, that'll give me time to catch up with Pea before it all kicks off."

They pulled up outside the hall's grand entrance five minutes later and were greeted by Percy who jogged down the front steps towards them.

He was thin, and tall like Mary, but with the bright red hair of his mother rather than her dark hair from her father's side. He had an angular but kind face that always seemed to be working itself into the next expression and gave the impression of constant motion. Mary had always thought he rather looked like a pencil and told him so frequently.

He was laughing as Mary opened the door and

stepped out onto the gravel.

"Mary!"

"Hi, Pea," she said embracing him. "So how is the hall? Not going to freeze to death, are we?"

"Nope! The plumbing's working again, thank God," he said laughing before his face clouded. "Had to sell another field off to do it though, one down by the village."

"You've got to do what you've got to do," Mary said, squeezing his arm.

"Oh, hello!" he said as Dot climbed out of the car. "If it isn't the ravishing Miss Tanner!"

Dot blushed a deep scarlet and shook her head. "Hello, Percy. Thanks for the invite."

"Did you hear that Mary? Proper manners." He pushed past her and gave Dot an overly flamboyant kiss on the cheek.

They turned to see Mary staring at them with her hands on her hips. "Am I going to have to throw a bucket of cold water on you two by the end of the weekend?"

"Oh, don't be such a grump, Mary" Pea said, embracing her and kissing both cheeks. He turned and ran back up the steps. "Come and get yourself in, it's freezing out here and I've got the fire lit! We'll sort the bags out later."

They followed him up the broad steps and into

Blancham Hall.

To Mary, the building had always had a slightly unreal quality since she had left it. As though she was visiting a museum dedicated to her past rather than the actual house she had grown up in. It was almost as though she was back on set, playing the role of her younger self.

Despite the grand name, the house wasn't as substantial as most English manor houses, and it had certainly seen better days. Its walls were pockmarked with age, its windows thin and draughty. And yet it was pleasing to the eye, like a comfortable piece of old furniture.

Wooden beams crisscrossed the high ceiling, dark oak furniture loomed against the white walls and the air was tinged with the musty weight of the years that hinted at a damp problem.

"I see the old place is still standing then?" Mary said, looking around the entrance hall.

"Of course it is! Just don't lean on anything." Pea laughed. "Have you eaten? I could get Hetty to make you something if you like?"

"You know I'd never turn down any of Hetty's cooking. How is she?"

"Same as ever, she'd like to see you I'm sure." Pea moved across to the right-hand wall where he tugged on a small velvet rope that vanished into the ceiling.

"You have servants?" Dot asked in surprise.

"Oh lord, no!" Pea laughed. "Hetty's just my lady from the village. She comes up and cooks when I'm having a do. Amazing woman, arms that could knead bread and kill a man in thirty seconds."

"And you'd be wise to remember that last one," came a voice from the far side of the hallway.

Mary turned slightly and looked at the shuffling figure of Hetty Wainthropp. No more than four foot ten, shaped like a rugby ball, and with a kind, rubbery face in which two mischievous eyes sparkled.

"I've told you before," she said, slapping Pea on the arm as she reached him. "I don't like it when you ring that bell for me. I'm not a bloody cow being called in for milking."

"Heaven forbid!" Pea said looking horrified at the thought.

"Well, if it isn't little Mary!" Hetty said, throwing her short arms as wide as they could go to embrace her.

"Hello, Hetty, how are you keeping?"

"Oh, not too bad, had a new hip, and every time it rains my knees stop working, but I don't complain."

Behind her, Pea rolled his eyes, suggesting that Hetty's complaining skills were almost as good as her cooking ones.

"I'm sorry to hear you won't be doing your show anymore," she continued. "I always liked watching you in that and I shan't watch it without you." She waggled her finger to emphasise the point.

"Thank you," Mary said, feeling suddenly emotional. "This is Dot," she said, hoping to move on before she cried.

"Nice to meet you, Dot," Hetty said. "Are you an actress an' all?"

"No, I was Mary's PA, now I'm just a friend."

Mary raised an eyebrow but said nothing.

"Well you're welcome here right enough," Hetty said before turning to Pea. "So, what did you want then?"

"I was just wondering if you could rustle something up for our guests?" Pea said sheepishly.

"Well, why didn't you say so?!" Hetty said, swiping him on the arm again. "You go and make yourselves at home and I'll bring you something lovely through."

She winked at Mary, turned, and waddled off the way she had come.

"Do you know?" Pea said leading the way. "If she wasn't such an absolute goddess in the kitchen, I'd have half a mind to hire someone with a little less feistiness about her."

"Don't be silly Pea," Mary said dismissively as

she followed him. "You'd lose a leg before you lost her apple crumble."

"Bloody hell, don't even joke about me losing her apple crumble," Pea said in a grave voice.

Mary laughed and headed through the door he had opened for her and Dot.

"Well this is lovely," Dot said as they entered.

Mary had to admit it was. The room was a long rectangle of high, corniced ceilings and dominated by a large fireplace on the left-hand wall. French doors lined the far wall and gave views across the estate, a piano and bar were situated at the end they had entered, and three huge sofas positioned in the centre, arranged around the fireplace and television.

This had been the main living space of the house for as long as she could remember. In her childhood, various rooms had become uninhabitable on and off due to leaks, damp and an assortment of other issues she had never really paid attention to. This room had always remained a warm oasis in winter and a stunning garden room in summer.

Pea moved over to one of the dark leather sofas and flopped onto it with one arm behind his head and his long legs crossed.

"So, Mary, what are your plans?"

"Plans?" Mary said confused. She was sitting on

the sofa opposite him, with Dot taking the place next to her.

"Now that you're not on the show anymore. What's next?!" He spread his arms wide, an encouraging smile on his lips.

"Oh, she thought she'd just wallow in her flat drinking gin in the middle of the day," Dot cut in before Mary could answer.

Mary pursed her lips at her in a threatening way before turning back to Pea. "I'm just taking some time to let the dust settle," she said firmly, wondering if she was trying to convince the others or herself.

"The dust's settled on you so much that you could be a museum exhibit," Dot muttered under her breath.

"Anyway!" Mary said loudly, hoping to put an end to this particular conversation thread. "Tell us who's coming tonight."

"Well," Pea said, leaning forward on the sofa and putting his elbows on his knees. "That's why I was wondering what you're doing next."

Mary noticed his eyes flicker to Dot momentarily, as though uncertain about something, before returning to hers. "Dot told me how you weren't getting much in the way of good offers,"

"Did she now?!" Mary said, staring daggers at Dot.

"You were the one complaining about Terry and his old people adverts!" Dot said defensively.

"Then I thought," Pea continued, oblivious. "Why don't I get back in the game and help an old friend out?"

"Back in the game? You don't mean you're going to sink more money into those awful sci-fi things, do you?" Mary asked, amazed.

Some years ago, when the family had been more solvent, Pea had decided he wanted in on the TV scene and had funded a small run of a sci-fi program that had quickly become the laughing stock of the country. In fact, it now enjoyed an almost cult following of people who found the low-budget effects and wooden acting hilarious. He had approached Mary at the time to be part of it, and she thanked her lucky stars every time she heard mention of the ghastly thing that she had said no.

"Oh no, this is going to be much more up your alley," Pea said, all seriousness. "A drama of some kind, you know, something you can get your teeth into."

"That's very kind of you, Pea," Mary said, the aforementioned teeth currently gritted. "But I don't need to take a charity job offer from my brother, thank you very much. Anyway, what on earth has that got to do with who's coming tonight?"

Pea frowned at her, clearly disappointed that she wasn't enthused by his idea.

"Well, I thought it might be a good idea to get a few people together who could be involved in the project. Steve Benz, Emily Hanchurch, Freddie Hale." Pea shrugged.

Emily stared at him, her mouth slightly open and her mind whirling over these three names. Steve Benz was a well-renowned TV director who she was acquainted with; Emily Hanchurch an award-winning writer; and Freddie Hale an actor, beloved by the nation and an annoying and immature man-child by anyone that actually knew him. Mary included. There was also the small issue of whom Freddie was dating.

"You do realise Freddie Hale is going out with Melanie Shaw, don't you?" she said bitterly.

"Oh," Pea said quietly, the smile freezing on his lips. "Um, no. But don't worry, I'm sure he's not going to be talking about her all evening."

"So, what you're telling me is that you've invited a crew and cast to this thing in order to persuade us all to be in your next big idea?"

Pea grinned at her and spread his hands, palm out towards her. "Not bad, eh?"

Mary turned to Dot. "I think we might have to review that rule on daytime drinking."

CHAPTER THREE

Mary finished the last mouthful of the cheese and cucumber sandwich Hetty had made her and washed it down with another sip of the potent gin cocktail Pea had produced.

She sighed at the words on the page in front of her. The magazine was fawning over the new star of *Her Law*, Melanie Shaw. The press loved her, of course they did. She was a goldmine for quotable quips and was a blonde bombshell to boot. The fact that she was now rumoured to be dating Freddie Hale only added to the stampede to crown her the new queen of British TV and the two of them the golden couple. She gave up on the words and instead stared at the large glossy picture that accompanied them in the magazine.

"I mean, she's just so bloody..." Mary waved her glass trying to think of the words.

"Young?" Dot offered from the sofa opposite her.

"Exactly," Mary nodded. "She's bloody young."

To Mary, it felt like all the media outlets in the world were about Melanie these days. Everywhere she turned she was reminded of how she had been traded in for a younger model, like a second-hand car that's body shape had suddenly gone out of fashion.

"It's not a crime to be young," Pea offered as he leaned forward and helped himself to another handful of nuts.

"No," Mary said sharply. "But apparently it's a crime to be old."

The doorbell rang out loudly from the hallway and Pea leapt from his seat.

"Here we go! The guests are arriving!"

"Whoopee," Mary said miserably.

She watched Pea skip across to the door on the far side and turned away towards the large windows and the view of the grounds stretching away beyond them.

"You need to stop being such a grumpy sod, Mary," Dot said. "Try and forget about all the nonsense with the show and just have a good time tonight."

"Don't think I haven't seen through your part in this little devious plan here, Dot," Mary countered as she fixed her with a fierce gaze.

"I don't know what you mean," Dot's eyes moved to her plain grey wool skirt, which she began to brush down distractedly.

"You know exactly what I mean. That you and Pea got together and concocted all this, didn't you? There's no way Pea came up with all this on his own. How would he even contact these people? You, on the other hand, would find it quite easy..."

"I was only thinking of what was best for you," Dot said defensively.

"Yes," Mary answered softly, feeling guilty. "Yes, of course, thank you for going out of your way of course, but come on! This was never going to work! You can't just throw some people together and expect a show to come out of it."

Laughter burst from the doorway making them both jump.

"Well then, I guess we're all wasting our time here then, aren't we?" a voice chuckled from the doorway.

Mary turned to see a short, round figure dressed in a dark blue suit which despite being clearly expensive, looked cheap on the man. She imagined that almost anything would. He had the kind of face that exuded cheapness, and no amount of Armani could cover it up. Mary had met him before, recognising with a shudder the look of lecherous smugness that seemed to permanently play on his toad-like face.

"Dave Flintock," Mary said in an unwelcoming tone.

"As I live and breathe!" Dave said, widening his arms. "How are you doing, Mary? Tough break you had." He plonked down on the sofa next to her, his face showing mock concern before turning back to his normal lopsided grin.

"What are you doing here?" Mary said bluntly, placing her drink back on the coffee table in front of her. "Percy didn't mention you were coming."

"Small oversight on his front I guess," Dave answered, the grin tightening. "I always go where my client needs me."

Mary frowned for a moment before making the connection. "Freddie Hale?"

"The one and only!" Dave laughed. "You're just as good a detective in real life as you are on the screen, Mary. Oh!" His hands moved to his face, which was locked in a mock horror. "Sorry when you *were* on screen that is." The grin returned instantly as Mary's hands balled into fists at her side. "You know, I could help with that in an instant," he said, sliding a card from his jacket pocket and holding it out to her.

"Oh," a voice from across the room said.

A willowy, red-haired woman hovered in the doorway, her rapidly blinking eyes staring at Dave Flintock.

"Hello, Emily," Dave answered with a leer. He rose from the sofa, moved across to her and kissed her on both cheeks, causing her body to go rigid with what looked like a mis of fear and repulsion. He took her arm and led her back to the sofa.

"This is Mary Blake, as I'm sure you know, and this is?" He frowned at Dot, as though seeing her for the first time.

"Dot Tanner, I'm Mary's friend."

"Right, Dot." Dave nodded. "This is Emily Hanchurch. Shall I go and rustle us all up some drinks?" He turned towards the bar in the corner without waiting or a reply.

Mary eyed the new arrival as she hovered, seemingly uncertain what to do. Mary had met her before, but she couldn't recall where or how. Over the years the various parties and functions she attended had melted into one.

"Nice to see you again Emily, have a seat here before he gets back," Mary said, patting the sofa to the right of her where she moved over to leave a gap.

"Thank you," Emily said appreciatively, realising that Mary had given her space where Dave Flintock could not sit next to her.

"Mary tells me you're a writer, Emily?" Dot asked. "Must be fascinating!"

"Oh, I don't know," Emily answered, looking over her shoulder nervously at the back of Dave. "I mostly just sit at home on my own, hunched over a keyboard." She shrugged and gave a nervous laugh.

"Don't worry about Dave," Mary said with a whisper. "His bark's much worse than his bite."

Emily gave a forced whimper of laughter, before looking down at her hands.

"Here we go, ladies!" Dave said, returning with four short, golden brown drinks that looked potent.

"Where's Pea got to?" Mary said, looking towards the door in hope that he would arrive and provide further dilution to Dave Flintock's presence.

"The others have all arrived by train at the station down the road. Percy went to pick them up." Emily answered.

"We don't need him to have a good time, do we ladies?!" Dave said, leaning back on the sofa next to

Mary and casually putting his arm around her. She elbowed him hard in the ribs making him spill half his drink onto his lap.

"What the bloody hell are you doing?!" he roared, standing.

"Reminding you to keep your dirty little paws to yourself," Mary said sternly.

He snorted, his round cheeks reddening. "You'd think in your situation you'd have the good sense to be nice to people like me who can help you out," he muttered before turning and heading towards the hallway in search of a bathroom.

"And you'd think that lecherous little worms like you would have died out in the Stone Age!" Mary called after him.

"The little weasel!" Mary said to herself, clutching her glass tightly.

"Come on, Mary," Dot said soothingly. "He's just trying to rile you. Ignore him."

"He is awful, isn't he?" Emily said next to her.

"I think you'll find most people in this industry are," Mary said bitterly.

"I've only met him once and..." Emily began before her pale cheeks suddenly reddened and she shook her head and took a sip of her drink, which made her cough and wince.

"You don't have to drink it," Dot said. "I'll make you something less toxic." She took the glass from her and headed over to the bar.

"I'm sorry," Emily said, eyes watering. "I'm not really used to hard drink."

Mary gave a small laugh, which she managed to turn into a cough as she realised that Emily was serious.

"What were you going to say about Flintock?" she asked by way of distraction.

"Oh, it's just that..." She looked over her shoulder towards the door, but there was no sign of the agent and so she continued. "It was a few months ago at some launch party or other. He said he could help my career and get me writing on some of the big shows if I 'played my cards right' and then he pinched me on the bottom!"

Mary sighed in sympathy. "He's an arse," she frowned and thought about this. "So, he must be compelled to pinch arse's on other people."

Mary had been lucky in her career. She had attended an open audition on a whim when on a shopping trip to London and, to her complete surprise, had landed the part. Within the week she had signed Terry Hope as her agent. At the time he had only had a few, small-time clients, but he had been a friend of a friend of her brother from school and so again she had found the easy route. But she was all too aware of how many sharks there were in the TV world, and Dave Flintock was a great white shark with sharp, bloodied teeth.

"I'm sorry you got replaced on your show," Emily said with a sympathetic smile.

"Oh, thanks," Mary sighed. "I guess it's all part of the business," she shrugged. "I just hate the reasons behind it. Just because a woman finds herself sagging in certain areas, it doesn't mean she's past it."

"Exactly the right attitude," Dot said as she returned with Emily's drink. "You need to get back out there and show them. There's no use crying over spilt milk," Dot added.

"I guess that rather depends on whether the milk in question is a perky little thing with annoyingly perfect hair."

There was a silent pause in the room.

"That doesn't make any sense," Dot said frowning.

"Sorry," Mary said. "I think I got a little lost in the metaphor there."

Voices sounded from the hallway. The high tinkle of a woman's laugh ringing out above them.

They looked up as Pea burst through the doorway, his eyes wide and flicking around the room until they landed on Mary.

"Mary, I'm sorry I didn't realise," he said rushing over to her.

"What is it?" Mary said, a prickle of fear rising up her spine at her brother's tone and pale face. His face was like an open book to her and right now PANIC was written in big bold letters.

"Just remember, I didn't know Freddie was dating her until you told me earlier!" Pea said, his face bright crimson.

Mary looked up at the door with a sudden sense of dread. A petite, blonde figure shimmied through the door. The golden ringlets of her hair fell perfectly on her shoulders, framing an angelic face.

"Oh!" the woman squealed, her hands clasping either side of her face. "Mary Blake! How exciting!" She rushed across to the sofa, perched next to Mary and took her hand. "I want to know everything about you! I simply have to do you justice when I start playing Susan Law!"

Mary's eyes glanced to Pea over Melanie Shaw's shoulder where he was standing, worry etched across his face.

"It's nice to finally meet you," Mary said, her eyes returning to Melanie's. Her voice was steady, even though her heart was pounding. It was taking all her strength not to run from the room and drive straight back to London.

"Do you know that you are one of my heroes?!" Melanie said with long eyelashes fluttering. "It is such an honour to be following in your footsteps."

"Oh, right," Mary answered feeling slightly bewildered.

"Oh yes, I've been a fan of yours since I was really little."

Mary forced a smile and nodded as inwardly her anger rose. She couldn't help but feel as though this was a deliberate dig at her age.

There was a moment of awkward silence as Melanie gazed at Mary with her large blue eyes, as though waiting for a reaction before more voices came from the doorway.

"Well, if it isn't Mary Blake!" a voice boomed from across the room. Freddie Hale wore a pale blue shirt that was open at least two buttons too many. White chinos finished at the ankle where his bare feet disappeared into a pair of cream loafers. To Mary's mind, he looked as though he was due to step onto a golf course rather than into a murder mystery weekend in November.

"Hello Freddie," Mary said rather weakly. She was getting the sinking feeling that this was going to be a long weekend.

"And would you look at this!" he said, opening his arms at Mary and Melanie on the sofa. "Last year's model sitting here with the new upgrade!" He laughed and then stopped, a false look of concern on his face.

"Oh, it's not awkward, is it?" he said dramatically before bursting out in laughter again.

"The only awkward thing in this room is your acting," Mary said, finding some of her old spirit lying under the pool of misery and gin inside her. She rose and moved past Freddie to where the final two guests had entered and were watching silently.

Steve Benz was a slight, ordinary man apart from his shock of white hair and pale skin. He had always given Mary the faint impression of a ghost, but a friendly one. In her brief run-ins with him over the years he had always come across as one of the nicer sorts you found in this industry.

"Hi Steve," she said, kissing him on both cheeks. "How are you?"

"You know, can't complain," he said shrugging.

Mary sensed an awkward silence building in the room and realised that all eyes were on her, waiting to see her reaction to Melanie being a guest here for the weekend. She was determined to show them that she wasn't a broken woman just yet.

"Right then, who thinks we should get nicely lubricated before we have dinner and start murdering each other?" she said more loudly than was necessary.

There was a smattering of laughter, punctured by the high ear-piercing giggle of Melanie Shaw.

Mary forced a grin onto her face and headed towards the small bar.

CHAPTER FOUR

"**A**nd that!" said Mary theatrically, "is how I know that you are the murderer!" She pointed an accusing finger at Pea who was grinning with the rather waxy appearance of someone who had had too much to drink.

"Oh, just wonderful!" Melanie squealed next to her. Mary forced a smile at her.

Three hours ago, Pea had begun by showing everyone to their rooms. Mary always felt strange being back in her childhood room, as though she was intruding on her younger self somehow, and the feeling hadn't changed when she had entered that large but rather damp smelling space she had once called home.

Once everyone had unpacked and poured

themselves further drinks, they had begun acting out the convoluted plot of the murder mystery evening Pea had arranged. With an increasingly drunken cast, there had been a not unrelated increase in good-will between all involved.

That is, apart from Melanie Shaw.

"See, she's not bad, is she?" Dot said as the various members of the play broke apart and headed either to the bar for a refill or to the sofas where they were sitting in front of the roaring fire.

"You are kidding me?" Mary said, looking at her in disbelief.

"No, why, what's wrong with her? I thought she'd been very nice to you?"

"Bloody hell, Dot, you really are clueless. She's not being nice to me, she's sticking the boot in whenever she can!"

Mary looked at the blank expression of her friend and was reminded that the subtleties of human interaction were not her forte.

"Listen," she said, putting her arm around Dot. "When she is saying how great I used to be when she was growing up and how the old shows really showed great energy and all that nonsense, what she's actually saying is that all of that stuff is missing from recent shows. She's also reminding me that I'm old and washed up."

"Are you sure?" she asked suspiciously.

"Yes! And have you seen her with Freddie? If those two are a legit couple then I'm a Peruvian taxidermist. She's as cold to him as haddock. When Pea showed them to their room, she insisted on them having separate rooms and Freddie didn't seem too happy about it. She's been teasing poor Emily about getting fired from her last job and there's something funny going on with her and Steve Benz."

"What do you mean?"

"Well, he's drinking like a fish and keeps trying to whisper to her for some reason and she keeps either muttering back to him or blanking him. All very mysterious if you ask me."

"Do you know?" Dot said, eyeing Melanie from across the room. "Now you mention it, I saw Dave Flintock and her arguing about something in the hall earlier on. Well," she said pausing with a frown, "at the time I thought they were arguing, but now I think about it, Melanie seemed to be quite calm and even smiling. Dave was bright red with anger about something though."

"She was probably winding him up like she is everyone else," Mary answered bitterly. "Oh, speak of the devil," she added as Melanie made her way across from the bar with a small tray of drinks.

"Here we go!" Melanie said, handing Mary a

flute of prosecco. "Pea says we're going to find out who the murderer is now, so I got us some bubbly." She turned to Dot who was standing with a stony look on her face. "Oh sorry, I didn't get you one! But then, servants don't get the bubbly do they!" She laughed in her high piercing giggle and turned away from them.

Mary watched Dot's eyes turn to stone, her jaw tense.

"Told you," she said softly, handing Dot her drink.

Obviously, Melanie had been referring to Dot's role in the murder mystery, but still. There had been something there that was suggesting Dot was Mary's servant in real life. She had called Percy "Pea" as well. No one other than Mary did that.

"Ok!" Pea shouted above the fifties' rock and roll that had been playing since they had finished dinner, Pea's favourite. "We have three more envelopes to read!" He moved around the room, handing one envelope to Steve Benz, who was standing with Emily Hanchurch, one to Freddie Hale, who hovered with his agent Dave Flintock, and one to Melanie.

"Oh, how exciting!" Melanie squealed, fanning her face with one thin hand.

"Now Steve, sorry, Alfonso, you get to open yours first!" Pea said excitedly.

Steve Benz, who was playing the role of Alfonso, took another large swig of whiskey from his tumbler and set it on the grand piano behind him. He opened the envelope and began reading. As a prime suspect in the murder, there was a slight tension in the air as everyone waited to see if he was about to confess. He didn't. Instead, the character of Alfonso explained how he, in fact, had an alibi for the crime, which let him off the hook.

Mary watched Steve Benz's pale, twitchy face as he stumbled through his lines. Something seemed off with him, as though his mind was elsewhere, and it wasn't anywhere good. She had noticed a closeness between him and Emily Hanchurch and had decided they would make a cute couple. She wondered if he was working up the courage to make a move and that was what was testing him.

Freddie Hale went next, delivering his lines with the usual flair and boyish charm that had endeared him to so many of the nation's housewives. His character was also innocent of the crime.

All eyes turned to Melanie.

"Oh my!" she cried when Freddie had finished. "Does this mean I did it?!"

"Why don't you open the bloody envelope and find out," Dave Flintock rumbled.

"Oh Dave, if you didn't want to join in, you shouldn't have trekked all the way out here just to spy on Freddie and me!" Melanie gave a short giggle and began opening the envelope.

Mary exchanged a meaningful look with Dot. Again, this was only a mild chastisement, just a meaningless retort really, yet there was something else behind it. A hidden, poisonous barb behind the sweetness.

Melanie began reading a confession of how she had committed the murder, shrieking and giggling with delight as she did so.

Mary scanned the eyes in the room.

Pea's were glassy from alcohol, but she had the impression he was actually listening to what Melanie's high voice was saying. He had enjoyed the whole murder mystery game, throwing his heart and soul into encouraging the others to take part and playing his own role with a gusto that more than made up for his lack of acting ability.

The eyes of the rest of the room told a different story.

Freddie Hale's were the hardest to read. His brow furrowed and his eyebrows knotted in what appeared to be fierce thought. There was emotion there as he stared at his Melanie, but whether it was love or maybe even hate, Mary couldn't tell.

Dave Flintock's emotions regarding Melanie Shaw were more obvious. His mouth was twisted into a foul sneer and his eyes glistened with alcohol and contempt.

Emily Hanchurch was perched on the stool of the grand piano, swaying slightly. Her eyes were set on Melanie, and a faint smile played upon her lips as though she was enjoying some private joke.

Steve Benz was standing silently, sipping at his whiskey, his face expressionless but his eyes sunken and sad.

Mary realised Melanie had finished reading and Pea had begun clapping. No one else joined in and he looked around bewildered.

"Well, maybe we should all have a nightcap and head off to bed, eh?"

"First sensible idea anyone's had all night," Dave Flintock grumbled.

"Well I thought it was tremendous fun," Melanie chuckled. "Just because Freddie's not going to be your golden ticket anymore, Dave, there's no need to take it out on everyone else."

"You jumped-up little..." Flintock began, stepping forward.

"Steady on, Dave," Freddie interjected.

Dave spun his glare towards him. "You haven't got a clue, have you?" he shouted. "She's spun you a load of crap and you've bought every line."

"I think maybe you should go to bed," Freddie said, his face reddening as he stepped in front of Flintock and puffed out his chest.

"You're bloody welcome to him, darling," Flintock jerked his thumb towards Freddie as he snarled at Melanie. He rose and glared at the both of them for a moment before storming out into the hallway.

"Well, there's nothing like a bit of drama to liven up the party!" Melanie giggled once the door had slammed behind him.

"Let's all just call it a night," Steve Benz said quietly.

"Oh!" Melanie laughed. "What a surprise, Steve Benz giving up on something."

Mary looked between them, shocked at this sudden outburst from Melanie, who seemed to have dropped any pretence of sweetness. She had spat Steve Benz's name as though it was an insult.

"I see you've been hanging around with Emily all night," Melanie said, smiling at the tall, red-haired woman next to him. "That will be a match made in heaven, a washed-up writer and a has-been director."

"Come on everyone!" Pea said hurriedly. "Let's all just try and get along, eh?" He looked at his watch and grinned. "I almost forgot! It's eleven!"

"And what's that got to do with anything?" Mary asked, wary of what Pea was going to make them all join in with next.

"It's my last little surprise!" he said triumphantly, "there's a meteor shower expected tonight, I thought we could all go up on the roof terrace and watch it." He gestured towards the heavens. "Come on, everyone, we can have our nightcap up on the roof! I got Hetty to make up some mulled cider!" He turned and headed out of the room with the rest of the group in tow, glad of a distraction from the sudden tension. He gathered everyone's coats from the large coat stand in the hallway and gleefully led them up the wide staircase like the pied piper, a broad grin plastered across his face.

Dave Flintock appeared from his room as they reached the landing to see what the commotion was and was soon persuaded by Pea to join the procession as he pretended to blow a trumpet using his hands and shouted: "Follow me!"

Although a terrible actor, there was something theatrical about Pea when he was on form like this, Mary mused.

"He's had too much to drink," muttered Dot from Mary's side as they followed him along the landing hallway to the far right-hand side where a door led into a winding stone staircase set into a narrow turret.

"Haven't we all?" Mary smiling wanly.

The roof of Blancham Hall had been a favourite play-place when they had been children. It had been a fort, a princess's tower and often just a place to escape from the world of adults.

As she emerged onto the familiar flat space, she felt a pang of nostalgia, which she forced down and tried to ignore as she always did with echoes of the past. She was suddenly aware of why she avoided coming back here as much as she should. These days it just reminded her of her mother, who was long gone, and her father, who might as well be. His mind lost in mist and his body becoming frail.

Pea led the group along the flagstone pathway between gravelled areas, and towards the central patio before spreading out to wind around the perimeter of the roof.

"I set a fire this afternoon and Hetty's made up a plug-in vat of mulled cider, which should be all ready," Pea said, fussing around the round black barrel that steamed gently in the dim light from yellow uprights dotted around the low wall at the edge of the roof.

There were murmurs of approval from the group as they gathered around the centre of the space where old iron furniture had been arranged in a circle around a large fire pit which Pea squatted next to, fiddling with a lighter that refused to work until Dave Flintock lit a cigar and handed his lighter to Pea.

Mary moved away to stand at the edge of the roof, looking out over the grounds and down to the river as she had done so many times before.

"You ok?" Dot said, arriving next to her.

"Oh yes, just reminiscing." Mary sighed. "No! Dot, don't! Mary shouted as her friend leaned forward on the battered stone parapet that ran along the top of the short wall. Dot jumped backwards as a stone tumbled down into the blackness beyond, with a puff of stone dust.

"Bloody hell Dot, look what you're doing!"

"Everyone alright?" Pea shouted from behind them.

"Fine," Mary called back.

"I did mean to mention," Pea continued, "the parapet is a bit dodgy I'm afraid, best to stay in the middle."

"Unlike you to not pay attention," Mary said to Dot as they turned back towards the group.

"Oh, sorry. My mind was just elsewhere."

"Like where?" Mary asked with a certain curiosity.

In the three years she had known Dot, she could count the times when she had been confided in on one hand. Dot was an excellent listener but was the queen of bottling up her own emotions.

"Oh, ignore me," Dot said shaking her head. "Just a bit tired probably."

"Still no movement down there?" Mary asked, glancing at Dot's midriff.

"No," Dot sighed. "I'll take the pills tomorrow."

"Come on, let's have a last drink before we turn in." She put her arm around her friend and guided her back towards the firelight where Pea was handing out hot mugs of cider and took two seats as they realised that the argument from earlier had now resumed.

"And tell me, Dave," Melanie said, "what exactly is it you're providing Freddie for this big fee of yours?" Her eyes glinted with malice in the firelight. She was sitting on a two-seater iron bench with Freddie Hale, while Dave Flintock, Steve Benz and Emily Hanchurch took individual seats in a circle around the fire pit.

"What do I provide?" Flintock snarled. "Only his whole bloody career! Before I came along, he was washing dishes in some rotten little pub!"

"Stop it, Dave," Freddie said, his voice low.

"Can you not see what she's bloody doing?!" Flintock moaned, spittle flying from his snarling lips. "She's playing games with you!"

"I rather thought that the game playing was your idea?" Melanie laughed.

Flintock snorted and leaned back in his chair, taking a large swig from the cider he clenched so tightly in his hand his knuckles had turned white.

"So," Pea said, in a voice that was clearly to imply that they should move on from whatever conversation had led them to this disagreement. "Steve, I hear you might have some new, exciting show in the pipeline?"

Steve Benz's eyes remained fixed on his drink as he answered.

"There's no new project."

"Oh," Mary said frowning. "What happened?"

"It just didn't work out," Steve answered with finality to his voice that made it clear the subject was closed.

Mary noticed as Emily's hand moved across to rest on Steve's, but he pulled away, leaving her cheeks draining of colour as she sipped at her cider.

Mary thought back to a couple of months ago when she had bumped into Steve Benz at a charity auction where he had enthused about a new prime time TV show he was going to be working on. He had been excited, energised and had seemed a different man to the morose one before her now.

"It just didn't work out," parroted Melanie. "That could be the story of your life, Steve, couldn't it? Maybe they could write that on your gravestone." She laughed with her grating, high-pitched laugh. The rest of the party looked around in an awkward silence.

"I think you should mind your manners," Emily Hanchurch said in a mouse-like voice.

"Ha!" Melanie roared. "So, she speaks, does she? I thought you were going to go the whole evening saying nothing other than the sweet nothings you've whispered to Steve there."

Emily's pale face flushed as she looked down at her lap. "I don't think you're a very nice person, Melanie," she said softly.

"Oh, darling!" Melanie laughed again. "There aren't any nice people, didn't you know that?"

"Oh, look!" Pea shouted in relief more than excitement. His right hand pointed to the sky and they all turned their heads towards the inky blackness. "There's was a shooting star, I think the shower is starting!"

They all stared up in silence as one, then two, then a whole range of bursts of light shot across the sky.

"It's beautiful," Mary said in wonder.

"Not as beautiful as a top-up would be," Melanie said. "Be a love, would you, Mary?" She waggled her glass towards her, a sickly smile on her bright red lips.

Mary resisted the urge to tell her where to stick it, and instead snatched the glass from her, turned and bent down to where the large, heated barrel of cider was positioned on the ground.

She had to be the bigger person here. Melanie was the type of person who thrived on getting under peoples' skins, but Mary wasn't going to give her the satisfaction.

As she watched the golden liquid trickle slowly from the tap on the side of the barrel, she noticed Dot's bag had toppled over behind her, spilling some of the contents onto the floor. She began putting the odd items back in, notepad, biro, compact mirror, pills. Her hand froze as she moved the pills towards the back and turned them over to see the label. These were the laxatives Dot was taking for her constipation. Before she even knew what she was doing, she pulled the silver foil tray from the packet and popped four into Melanie's cider before stuffing the packet back in the bag. Her heart pounding, she got up and turned back towards the group, leaning across and handling Melanie her drink.

"Can I get anyone else a top up?" she asked feeling slightly giddy. There was a chorus of affirmatives and she got to work as a distraction from her childish act of revenge.

CHAPTER FIVE

It was only twenty minutes later when Mary noticed the first signs that her impulsive act was having an effect.

Melanie had become quiet. The snide comments and remarks that she had been firing in all directions throughout the evening were suddenly halted. She had sunk back into her chair, her hands lightly resting on her stomach.

A few minutes later there was a whispered conversation between Melanie and Freddie, which resulted in his twinkling eyes turning to Pea.

"Percy, I think we're going to turn in for the night. Melanie's not feeling well."

"Oh! Of course," Pea jumped up from his seat ready to escort his guests.

"Don't be ridiculous, Freddie," Melanie croaked.

She got up unsteadily and turned towards Pea. "We've got separate rooms remember, I just want to go to bed."

"Right, well I hope you feel better in the morning," Pea said, awkwardly glancing over her shoulder at Freddie, who was looking as though someone had slapped him across the face.

Mary watched her leave with Pea escorting her. Rather than feeling the pang of guilt she had expected, she had to reach her hand to her mouth to stifle a giggle.

"What's got into you?" Dot said quietly next to her.

"Oh, nothing," Mary said, sipping at her cider in order to give her lips something to do other than to grin.

"Freddie, you need to wake up to that woman," Dave growled, leaning towards his client, elbows on knees.

"Just leave it will you, Dave." Freddie slumped back in his seat, looking for all the world like a moody teenager.

"Well," Emily said, smoothing her skirt down with one hand. "I hope she feels better in the morning."

"You might just be the only one, love," Flintock muttered darkly.

Freddie huffed and strode off across the rooftop.

"I don't know how he puts up with her," Mary said watching him go.

"You don't know the half of it," Flintock said. There was a pause from the rest of them, but he said no more.

"I think that's it for the meteor shower," Pea said as he emerged back onto the roof from the door into the house.

"Oh, don't worry," Mary said. "I think we've had enough fireworks here to keep us entertained even without the meteor shower, to be honest."

"That woman," Steve Benz said in a low voice that instantly caught the attention of everyone, "has grown up to be the devil."

There were a few moments of silence before Pea chimed in.

"Right, I think I might call it a night."

"Good idea," Mary said yawning. She suddenly felt thick exhaustion fall on her like a blanket. As though Pea's words had been a trigger for unconsciousness.

"Me too," Dot said, "it's getting late."

Mary watched Pea look around the group expectantly, but no one else replied.

"Ok, well, there's more mulled cider if you want it and plenty more wine and spirits downstairs."

"Good," grunted Flintock as he rose and moved to the mulled cider barrel once again.

Mary, Pea and Dot said their goodnights and headed back down the stairs.

"Well, Pea," Mary said. "I wouldn't say that was one of your finest social gatherings."

"No," he grinned sheepishly. "Sorry about all this. Thought it was going to be good for you."

"You mean you thought you could fix everything for me by just throwing some horrible people together?"

"Something like that, yes."

"His heart was in the right place, Mary, it's not his fault that Melanie turned up." Dot said next to them.

"Oh, I know," she replied, sagging with a sudden exhaustion. "Thanks anyway, Pea," she squeezed his arm as she kissed him on the cheek. "Anyway, I'm shattered, night."

They both bid her goodnight as she headed into her room. She realised she had meant to ask Pea whether Hetty was coming back in the morning to make breakfast for everyone and turned back towards the corridor.

She opened the bedroom and stepped out into the hall to see Dot and Pea talking at the other end as they entered Pea's room.

What on earth were those two up to? Surely not...

She moved down the landing, without thinking what she would do when she caught up with them. As she reached the far end, she slowed as something in the tone of the voices she could hear through the open door gave her pause to think. Their hushed tones, their urgency, filled her with a nervousness that took her by surprise. Whether it was the dim light, the old and creaky house, or just the time of night, she found herself not walking towards the voices of old friends with a light heart. Instead, she crept forwards secretively, ears straining to hear what they were saying.

"We're going to have to say something." She heard Dot say, her voice floating through the opening of the door. "I don't like lying to her."

"You're not lying to her, you're just not telling her everything," Pea replied. "Look, I just want to look into things a bit first. There's no point upsetting her over nothing."

"And you still have no idea what he meant about this fool's bottom business?"

"Not a clue, no. It could just be a load of nonsense."

"Sometimes these things can have a grain of truth though, and she'd never forgive you if she found out you'd lied later. I think we should talk to her tomorrow," Dot said firmly.

Mary heard Pea sigh.

"Fine, I'll talk to her."

"Good."

A cold shiver ran down Mary's spine. How could this be? Dot and Pea were acquaintances, nothing more. Now they had secret meetings where they discussed keeping something from her?

She tried to ignore the pounding of her heart and focus on what they were saying.

"Tonight was obviously a disaster," Dot continued. "But I appreciate the effort. I'm not sure what's going to happen if she doesn't get back into something soon."

There was a moment of silence from the other side before she heard movement, turned and scurried back along the corridor. As she reached her room, no one had emerged from the door at the other end, but she decided not to go back and eavesdrop again.

A few minutes later and Mary was in her childhood bed, tucked up under a heavy duvet and feeling again like a child whose parents were off deciding what was best for her.

She was grateful to Pea for trying to get her back into the TV game so soon, but it had made her realise something that had taken her by surprise. Instead of seeing these people as an opportunity, they had only reminded her of all the things she hated about the industry she had spent so much of her life in.

Instead of seeing Dave Flintock as an agent who could maybe offer her more than her current one, she saw him as a shark. Only in it for himself and treating his clients like dirt.

She didn't see Emily Hanchurch as a successful writer who might be persuaded to pen something with her in mind, rather she had seen her as a mousy, quiet woman who had obviously been walked all over by producers and actors alike for her whole career and had now had any fight or spirit she had ever had, knocked out of her.

And Steve Benz who had looked so alive and full of excitement when she had last seen him, had been cynical and sour. Was he sullen and sulky because his dream project was in ashes, or was there something else going on there?

Then there was Freddie Hale and Melanie Shaw. Melanie was the spoilt and manipulative person she had always imagined her to be, which was something of a comfort. It would have been far worse if she had actually turned out to be nice. Mary wasn't sure she could have handled that.

Freddie Hale seemed to fit right in alongside her, though their relationship was odd at best. He seemed to be the doting boyfriend, but she seemed to enjoy keeping him at arm's length.

Mary sighed in the dark. Maybe she had had enough of the whole TV game, maybe it was time for something new, but what on earth would that be? She had no skills other than pretending to be someone else.

And then there was that conversation between Dot and Pea. What on earth were they keeping from her? And why did they think she couldn't handle it?

As her mind tumbled and turned over, the rising wind whistled through the loose and ancient windows, gently lulling her into sleep.

CHAPTER SIX

M ary woke with a start and looked around the room in a panic. There was nothing there, but she strained her ears as she heard a faint tapping noise, noticeable even above the wind that still whined outside. She swung her legs from the bed and cocked her head trying to determine the direction it was coming from, but it promptly stopped.

A thin layer of sweat covered her body despite the cool air of the room. Her mouth was so dry it felt as though it might catch fire from friction with every movement of her jaw.

She really shouldn't have drunk so much.

She turned, flicked on the bedside lamp and rubbed her eyes. Eventually, she focussed on the dark oak surface and realised with annoyance that she had failed to bring water to bed and there were no glasses in the room to fetch any from the bathroom.

Mary lay back down, picturing just how far away the kitchen was and groaned inwardly when she heard a new noise, this time like a soft thump. This bloody old creaking house she thought bitterly, pulling the covers over her head. She closed her eyes and tried to prevent her mind from again filling with questions over her future when a noise from the corridor outside made her eyes snap open again. The noise was the creak of a floorboard, possibly someone with more drive to reach the kitchen than she had.

She lay back and stared up at the ceiling, just visible from the light that bled under the door. She realised with a sinking feeling that she wouldn't get back to sleep now without getting some water and so pulled back the heavy duvet and swung her legs over the edge of the bed. Grabbing her dressing gown from the back of the door, she headed out into the corridor. Her eyes flicked towards Pea's room at the other end of the hall, but the door was now closed. Dot had clearly returned to her room and there was no sign of anyone else.

She made her way down the wide staircase, which groaned underfoot like a sleeping bear, reached the bottom of the stairs and turned left. She moved across the hallway towards the back wall where a discreet door was set into a green baize panel, a remnant from days long before her time there, when servants had dealt with the cooking.

The kitchen was a large, functional space. Divided down its length by a metal-topped bench with matching benches running along either wall.

Mary set to work, opening the third cupboard on the right and taking a glass before pouring herself a drink from the tap. She gulped at it greedily, feeling her throat return to some kind of normality as she shivered slightly in the chill of the room.

What had Dot meant by saying, "she wasn't sure what would happen" if Mary didn't get back to work soon? Did she think that Mary was some sort of emotional wreck that was going to crumble without the high-profile role she had become so used to?

She felt a pang of concern run through her as she pictured herself back in her flat in London, sprawled on the sofa, with a glass of gin and tonic nearby. Damn it, maybe Dot was right.

A noise behind her made her spin around, sloshing water across the flagstone floor.

"Well, hello, Mary," Dave Flintock said grinning. He wore a dressing gown that was worryingly short, and not large enough for his ample belly. The shining silk fabric stretched around his protruding gut and finished just above his surprisingly thin and knobbly knees.

"What the bloody hell are you doing?!" Mary snapped, "You frightened the life out of me!"

"Couldn't sleep," he said shrugging. "Maybe you and I could keep each other company for a while?" He grinned, moving towards her, his hand snaking towards the gown that covered her breasts.

She slapped him hard across the face and brought her knee up at the same time, doubling him over in pain as he fell softly to the floor.

"Go to bed, Flintock," she said, her voice like steel. She grabbed her glass of water and strode out, leaving him groaning softly on the flagstones.

She was heading back up the stairs when a movement above caught her eye. Emily Hanchurch was rushing along the hallway, her long pale legs flashing in the dark from under her dressing gown. She stopped at a door and knocked. The door opened almost immediately to reveal Steve Benz, who ushered her in before closing the door. There was no mistaking the intention there, thought Mary.

She began climbing the stairs and as she reached the top, another door opened and a figure emerged.

"Oh, hi, Mary," Freddie Hale said as he approached her. "Just thought I'd see if Melanie was ok, she had a bit of a dicky tummy earlier."

"Oh, right," Mary said, hoping he couldn't see her blush in the gloom. "Well, I hope she's feeling better. Night Freddie." She turned away as he knocked on Melanie's door and called her name, stepped into her room and locked the door behind her.

Who knew there was so much activity after dark? she sighed to herself before crawling back into bed and once again falling into a restless sleep with various visions of her unknown future tumbling through her mind.

CHAPTER SEVEN

Mary woke to a room transformed from its appearance in the night. Golden light filtered through the embroidered curtains and bathed everything in a warmth that could not help but raise a smile, even with her head feeling as though it was full of cotton wool. As a child, she had loved the glow this room had had in the mornings.

Her thoughts were derailed by the recollection of Dot and Pea's concern that she would go off the rails without the focus of her job, and the truth they seemed to be keeping from her. Rather than face this with worry as she had done last night, the morning light seemed to have filled her with new vigour. She would show them that she was more than just an actress whose career was on the slide. She would find

out what on earth their little hushed conversation
had been about, and she would reinvent herself too.
As what? She didn't know, but even that unknown
only seemed exciting, rather than daunting.

She hopped out of bed and moved to the en suite
bathroom with its antiquated plumbing and sang to
herself as she showered.

A few minutes later and she was stepping out
into the hallway where Freddie Hale was standing a
couple of doors down, rapping his knuckles on the
solid wood in front of him as he had been when she'd
retired for bed.

"Have you been there all night, Freddie?!" Mary
laughed, thinking of him gently knocking for
Melanie in the early hours.

"No," he said, his face set in grim concern.
"Melanie wouldn't answer me last night, so I gave up,
but she's still not responding."

Mary looked at her watch. "Well, it is only nine."
She shrugged.

"I don't care what bloody time it is," Freddie
snapped, "I want to know she's OK!"

As she looked at this overgrown boy, Mary felt a
little sympathy for Freddie. Being in a relationship
with Melanie Shaw would be enough to send anyone
crazy. It occurred to Mary that maybe Melanie
simply didn't want to see Freddie. She moved down

the hall to him and knocked on the door herself as he stepped aside.

"Melanie? It's Mary. Can you just let us know you're alright?"

There was no sound from the other side of the door.

"It's locked, I've already tried it," Freddie said as Mary tried the handle. "I'm going to break it down."

"Now, just wait a minute," Mary said, holding her hand out flat to stop Freddie advancing on the door. "Let's go and ask Pea first, it's his house after all."

She realised as she spoke that there was a part of her that was annoyed about this. Of course, she hadn't really wanted anything to do with the place after her father had gone, but, still, it had been her home once too, and now it was Pea's alone. Despite the money she had regularly contributed to its upkeep, this was no longer the family home. Maybe this was why she avoided coming here now?

"Anyway," she continued, "maybe he's got some sort of master key or something."

She turned and walked the length of the hallway to the far end of the corridor to Pea's room. She rapped on the door until she heard moaning from inside.

"Bloody hell!" She heard Pea exclaim. "What the hell's going on? Is there a fire or something?!"

"Just open the door, Pea," Mary shouted. "It's an emergency."

She listened to the muffled sounds of swearing from the other side until a dishevelled, hastily dressed Pea emerged with a pale face and an annoyed frown.

"What's the matter?!" he said, running his hand through his uncombed hair.

"Melanie's locked in her room and she's not answering her door."

"So? She's probably just a heavy sleeper or something."

"Have you got another key to the rooms?"

"Of course I haven't!" Pea said, "I haven't turned the place into a hotel!"

"You know, that's not a bad idea. Anyway, Freddie's about to barge the door down unless you can think of something else?"

He leaned around her and looked down the corridor to where Freddie was still thumping on the door. The other guests were beginning to appear from their rooms. Emily Hanchurch, Mary noted, appeared from her own room, which was past Melanie's, and not Steve Benz's. Steve himself appeared from his room with Dave Flintock and Dot following closely from theirs.

"What's happening?" Dot asked, bustling to the front next to Mary and Pea.

"Melanie's locked in and she's not replying," Mary answered.

"She's probably just hungover and sleeping it off," Flintock grumbled. He was the only one of the group who was dressed and a part of Mary's brain that wasn't preoccupied with the situation breathed a sigh of relief at not having to see him in his silk robe again.

"Percy," Freddie said turning to pea who was rubbing his eyes and clearly still trying to wake up. "I need to break the door down, she was feeling ill last night and anything could have happened."

"Yes, of course," Pea answered miserably, rubbing his forehead. "If we have to."

As Mary watched Freddie walk back to take a run up, she became aware of a rising sense of panic in her chest. A few laxatives couldn't actually harm someone, could they? It was only a couple over the recommended dose. Then again, what if it had reacted with some other medication she had been on that Mary didn't know about? She gripped the front of her dressing gown tightly as Freddie ran at the door, threw his shoulder into it and bounced back across the hallway, landing with a soft moan.

Flintock burst out laughing before catching himself and asking his client if he was ok. Freddie muttered an expletive and pulled himself up rubbing his shoulder.

"These are solid oak doors," Dot said moving to the doorway and peering down at the lock. "You'll probably break your shoulder before you break this door down."

"Shall we call a locksmith?" Emily asked anxiously.

"No need," Mary said before reaching up and pulling a hairpin from Dot's tight bun. She was now desperate to get inside herself and see what horrors she had caused to Melanie's digestive system.

"Hey! What on earth are you doing?" Dot exclaimed as her hair fell about her shoulders.

"Has anyone got a sheet of paper?" Mary asked ignoring her.

"I've got some on the desk in my room," Pea said as he stared at Dot. He tore his gaze from her before hurrying off to get it.

"Are you alright?" Emily said, crouching next to Freddie and looking at his shoulder.

"Fine," Freddie said irritably, pulling away and

standing up. "You're not seriously suggesting you're going to be able to pick the lock, are you?" he said irritably.

"No," Mary said, her mind whirring, "because there's no need to."

She took the sheet of paper from Pea as he returned and slid it under the doorway.

"These doors are thick, but they're old and there's a decent gap at the bottom of them," she continued as she took the hairpin and moved it to the lock. "So, all I need to do is push the key out." The clanging of metal on wood rang out from the other side of the door. "And then pull the paper out," she finished, doing as she said and removing the paper, on which rested the key.

Freddie moved down and snatched it up, ramming it into the lock and throwing open the door in a flash.

There was a collective gasp from the small group huddled around the doorway.

There, in the middle of the room, lay Melanie Shaw, a small pool of blood haloed around her head.

"Oh my god!" Freddie said, his weight falling against the door frame.

Dot rushed forward and bent over the still form of Melanie Shaw.

"She's dead," she said coolly. "Somebody phone the police and nobody else come into the room."

"I'll call," Pea said in a shaky voice, walking down the hallway to his bedroom.

"The window's open," Steve said pointing. The group's eyes moved to the window on the far side of the room where the curtains were flapping in the cool morning breeze.

"It has been a while," Dot said, "it's bloody freezing in here." She got up and made her way back to the door."

"Do you think someone broke in?" Emily said in a horrified voice.

"I'm not sure," Pea replied. "It would be one heck of a climb up from the outside, she probably fell and hit her head on something. Come on, I think everyone should go downstairs and have a cup of tea. We need to leave everything just as it is for the police."

There was a muttering of agreements, mostly from people in a state of shock. Mary, on the other hand, was locked in a guilty silence. Could the pills she had given Melanie have caused her to become woozy enough that she would fall and fatally hit her head? She had no idea, but the thought was twisting her stomach into knots. Freddie was leaning against the wall, his eyes wide, his cheeks drawn and pale.

"Come on," she said to him, taking his arm and turning him away from the door.

"I don't understand," he said shaking his head.

"None of us do," Mary said patting his forearm, "let's just get you sitting down with a cup of tea."

Which I need as much as you, Mary thought.

CHAPTER EIGHT

M ary cradled a cup of tea in her hands and watched from across the room as Dot talked to a uniformed officer. She appeared calm, business-like, as if this were just some small issue at work.

Mary had seen her friend in this mode many times over the years, but never when a dead body had been involved. Mary found her efficiency a little disconcerting given the circumstances.

"I can't believe this has happened here," Pea said next to her on the sofa. "Do you think I'll be charged with manslaughter?"

"Oh, don't be silly Pea," Mary chided. "It wasn't your fault, accidents like this could happen anywhere at any time." She took another sip of tea, her hand shaking slightly. She was trying to convince herself more than anyone. Hoping against hope that the laxatives she had given her the night before had not had an effect that had led to Melanie's death.

"Yes, I guess so," he sighed. "I just can't help feeling at least partly responsible. I know the place is a bit rough around the edges, but I didn't think anyone would get hurt like this."

Mary frowned as the scene that had confronted them in Melanie's room flashed across her mind.

"How big is that room do you think, Pea?"

"Which room? Melanie's? Oh, pretty big as bedrooms go. Why?"

"I'm just wondering about where she was when we opened the door," Mary said looking up at the vaulted ceiling in thought.

"What do you mean?"

"Well, if she fell down and banged her head, she must have hit it on something right?"

"Right."

"Well, what was it? She was laying almost in the middle of the room, her head was about as far away from any piece of furniture as she could be."

Pea paused before answering. "Maybe she fell, hit her head, and then crawled out into the middle of the floor?" Pea said looking back at her.

"Maybe," Mary said in a doubtful voice. "I need

some fresh air," she said suddenly. She rose and placed her teacup on the coffee table in front of her, noticing that she had now caught the attention of the rest of the group who were sitting in various chairs around the space.

"Where are you off to?" Flintock asked, apparently annoyed with the entire world.

"I'm just going to get some fresh air," Mary replied.

"I don't think the police will like it if you leave," Steve Benz said, frowning.

"Oh, I won't go far," Mary said dismissively before moving towards the doorway.

She felt Dot, and the officer she was talking to, turn towards her as she passed them.

"Mary?" Dot said, her face full of concerned questioning.

"I just need some fresh air for a minute."

"I'm afraid no one can..." The officer stopped talking mid-sentence. Mary recognised the familiar face of someone who has just seen someone from one of their favourite TV shows.

"Oh, Miss Blake. Well, I'm sure a few minutes won't hurt, please don't go too far though."

Mary gave him a quick smile and left before Dot could offer to join her. She headed out of the main hall and into the crisp morning air. A thin layer of mist clung to the green grass that sloped away in all directions, but the sky itself was becoming bluer by the minute as the strengthening sun burned off the haze of the morning. The wind that had risen in the night had vanished and left the morning still and calm.

She glanced at the multiple cars in the driveway, now joined by two police cars and turned left, making her way along the front of the building

She had not wanted to turn right, as it would have brought her past the windows of the sitting room where the rest of the group would have seen her. She past the tall library windows and ran her eye over them to ensure that everything was as it should be before she reached the corner of the house and turned left again.

Ahead of her, just visible through the haze, a church steeple peered through the distant trees. She again felt the nostalgic pang of these places that reminded her so much of her childhood.

As a family, they had often walked down to Bloxley village and enjoyed a pint in the pub, The Gardiner's Arms. That had been before, when her mother had been alive and her father's mind still as sharp as a tack. She shook her head to clear her thoughts. She needed to focus on what was happening now. There was a reason she had come out here, and she needed to see for herself.

She rounded the corner of the building and began looking up. Her eyes landed on the row of first-floor windows and mentally counted along until she was sure she had reached Melanie's. Her room, she knew, was the only one other than Pea's on the far side of the building to have two windows, being larger than the others, so she counted three across to find the window to Melanie's room. This was confirmed as she spotted a uniformed officer pass across the still open window frame. She moved to the wall underneath and looked upwards.

The wall was a sheer and unforgiving surface. Apart from a few areas of crumbling mortar, there were no signs of easy handholds or things to climb. She looked along the wall until she saw an iron drainpipe that ran from the ground to the flat roof above. If someone had scaled it, they might have been able to make it to the window adjacent, but it was two more windows across to Melanie's room. Unless the attacker was a veritable trapeze artist and able to leap from windowsill to windowsill, Mary couldn't see how they could possibly have climbed up there. Even then, there was the question of how they could have climbed down again.

"Doesn't look like someone could make it up there, does it?" a voice said from behind.

Mary spun around and her big toe thwacked into something solid, sending her sprawling on the grass.

"Are you ok?" the voice said, as a strong hand took her arm and helped her to sit up.

She looked up into a pair of large brown eyes, which stared out from beneath a mop of curly hair the same colour. They were soft, kind eyes with a mischievous twinkle to them and laughter lines that instantly warmed her to him.

"I'm fine," she said, leaning down and rubbing her foot. "I just stubbed my toe on something. She looked around and saw a large lump of curved stone lying in the grass. "This whole bloody place should come with a health warning," she muttered as she got up, wincing as she put weight on her toe.

The man's arm reached around her waist to steady her.

"Thank you, I'm fine," Mary said rather more sternly than she had meant to. He retracted his arm and instead offered his hand.

"I'm Inspector Corrigan,"

"Nice to meet you," she said taking his hand. "Mary Blake."

"Don't worry, I know who you are, Miss Blake."

"I think that would be unlikely, bearing in mind

we haven't met," she answered. "Maybe you just know *of* me."

"Ok, fair point," he said nodding. He studied her for a moment before turning and looking up towards the window as she had done just a few minutes before.

"So, you wondered if someone could have got up there as well, did you?"

"Yes, it's impossible." She answered, adjusting her feet to place her weight on her left foot as the toe on her right still throbbed.

"Nothing's impossible Miss Blake, but I admit it seems implausible."

He had a northern twang to his deep voice that made his speech almost lyrical and was certainly pleasant on the ear.

"I find it interesting that you are out here, though?" he said turning back to her.

"Oh, why?"

"On your show, you play someone who solves crimes, do you not?"

"Yes," she answered slowly.

"And here you are, trying to solve another one."

"Well, not really. I just wanted to…"

"I'm sure I don't need to remind you that there is quite a difference between the fictional world of policing and the real one?"

"Inspector," Mary said testily. "I have this morning discovered a dead body and unsurprisingly needed some air. I stepped around the back as I was curious how someone could have climbed up to the window, yes, but that is all."

"I see," he smiled, "and when you discovered the body, did you notice anything?"

"What do you mean?"

"Well, I assume you noticed that the victim had sustained a head injury?"

"Yes, that part was rather obvious," Mary said sarcastically.

"And presumably you saw that the window was open and so you came around here?"

"Yes, what exactly is your point, Inspector?"

"Well, I'm just wondering why you didn't assume she hadn't just fallen and hit her head."

Mary felt the prickle of heat running up the back of her neck. She knew the chain of events was obvious, but she didn't want to believe it because it might have meant that her prank had had something to do with another person's death. No matter how vile Melanie Shaw had been in life, no one deserved that. There was no way though, that she wanted to convey this to the inspector.

"When we saw her she seemed to be lying with her head in the middle of the floor and I thought it was strange that she wouldn't be next to whatever she hit her head on," she said, desperate to give any reason other than the true one in the face of these searching brown eyes of the law.

"A very good observation," Corrigan nodded. "Of course, she may have crawled into the middle of the room from where she hit her head?" he said, looking at her questioningly.

"I couldn't see any trail of blood, it looked like she had died just where she had fallen."

"Well, I certainly don't think those years of solving crimes on TV were wasted on you, Miss Blake. I had exactly the same thoughts, and that was before I had looked over all the furniture with edges that might be able to cause a wound like that and found no obvious sign of any blood, hair or skull fragments. Of course, the crime scene folks might turn up something, but it looks unlikely."

Mary looked from his face, up to the window and back again.

"But what on earth do you think happened to her, then?"

"At the moment, I don't know," he said in a low, serious voice, "but you can be damn sure I'm going to find out. Can I walk you back to the sitting room? I'd like to get going on witness statements and I'd prefer everyone in one place."

"Of course," Mary said in a daze. She set off back to the house hobbling.

"Please, allow me," he said, offering his left arm to her. She gratefully took it and with him taking her weight, they headed back around the outside of the house towards the front entrance in silence.

CHAPTER NINE

"What on earth possessed you to go around the back and start looking at the window?" Dot said in an admonishing tone. "You're not actually Susan Law you know, out there to solve crimes."

"Oh, bloody hell!" Mary said rolling her eyes. "Not you too. I told you, I just wanted some fresh air and ended up around the back of the house and then thought I'd see if I could work out how someone might have got up there."

"She must have just banged her head," Pea said.

"I'm not so sure," Mary said slowly.

"Why's that?" Dot said, square eyebrows arching.

The three of them were standing in a huddle at the far end of the sitting room by the tall windows that looked out across the grounds.

"Did you see where she was when Pea opened the door?" Mary said, turning to Dot, again desperate to find any other narrative than that of Melanie being affected by the pills she had given her. "She was nowhere near any of the furniture, and I didn't see any blood anywhere around the body."

"Mary," Dot said in a shocked whisper. "Think about what you're saying, last night we were all sitting around having drinks with her and now you're referring to her as 'the body', what's got into you?"

"Nothing," Mary said defensively, "just slipping into language from the show, I guess. Anyway, Inspector Corrigan has told me that it doesn't look like there's any trace of blood on any of the furniture so where exactly do you think she hit her head?"

"But no one could have climbed that wall, could they?" Pea asked.

"I don't think so, no," Mary admitted.

"So, what exactly are you saying?" Dot asked, looking at her curiously. "That someone floated through the door into that bedroom, hit her over the head and then floated back out again?"

Mary's reply though was unheard as an officer called out from the doorway to the hall.

"We're ready for you, Miss Blake," the young man said, smiling in a way that Mary guessed was meant to be reassuring.

"Back in a bit!" she said to her friends, hoping to sound jovial and light-hearted, though the truth was that she felt anything but.

Everyone else had already given their statements, Mary had been saved for last. Was this because she had already spoken to Inspector Corrigan? Or was it because somehow they already suspected that she had something to do with it? Surely, they couldn't have found the laxatives in her system that quickly?

She was led across the hall to a door on the opposite side, which led to the dark, book-lined study that had been her father's domain for so many years. She knew Pea used it now, but to her, it would always be her father's room. And the last place she would want to be. A shiver ran down her spine as she stepped into the gloomy space. What little light there was came from a glass-shaded lamp, which was positioned on the large leather-topped desk to the left. Inspector Corrigan sitting behind it scribbling in a black notebook.

"Ah, Miss Blake, please take a seat." He gestured to the seat opposite him and Mary took it, as the officer closed the door behind her and standing with his back against it. "Your brother has been kind enough to allow us to set up in here for the time being, but I realise this was your family home too, so please tell me if you have any objections."

Mary shrugged.

"So," Corrigan continued, "would you like to take us through what happened last night and this morning?"

Mary nodded and began.

She described everything as it had happened during the evening, leaving out only her own indiscretions with the laxatives and the secret meeting between Dot and Pea she had witnessed, deciding that there were some things best left unsaid, even in a murder enquiry.

"And what do you think Mr Flintock was doing wandering the house so late at night?" Corrigan asked when she reached the point where she had met the agent in the kitchen.

"I've no idea, but he made it pretty clear what he *wanted* to do," she said with disgust. "I slapped him, kneed him in the groin and went back to bed."

Corrigan stifled a laugh with a cough and pretended to look intently at his notes.

Mary smiled. Clearly the inspector had not enjoyed his time with Dave Flintock either.

For Mary, men had either been friends or lovers, but rarely both. There had only ever been one man she had become close to, but his career had taken him to America and after a few transatlantic trips, the fire had fizzled out. She had found solace in shallow encounters with younger men, of which there were plenty in the acting scene of London. Lately, though, she had felt the years weighing more on her, and companionship beyond that of the fussing Dot seemed to have some appeal.

"And you didn't see anyone else on your way?" he continued.

"I did, actually. I saw Emily Hanchurch going into Steve Benz's room, and Freddie Hale was knocking on Melanie's door."

Corrigan showed no reaction, and Mary guessed the other guests had already mentioned their whereabouts to him.

"And can you think of anyone who might have had reason to harm Melanie Shaw?"

He stared at her straight-faced, but there was that twinkle in his eye again which suggested he knew exactly what he was saying.

"You're joking, surely?"

He shrugged and gestured with both palms facing upwards.

"Well, I think most people would have had some reason to hate Melanie Shaw. If they'd met her that is."

"And that would include you would it, Miss Blake?"

Mary took a deep breath. "I don't think it's any

secret that Melanie has replaced me on the show *Her Law*."

"It's not," he said, watching her. He had a way of being able to stare at her so intently that she felt as though he was boring through into her mind and reading it as clearly as if it were spray-painted on the wall. "My mother, for one, was very disappointed. And what about the others here tonight?"

Mary opened her mouth at this reference of his mother's fandom, but then decided against and instead shrugged. "Melanie wasn't exactly an easy person to like," she said diplomatically.

"But you didn't notice anything in particular that stood out to you?"

She thought of the strange hurried arguments between Freddie and Melanie, of Dave Flintock's fury at the young actress, and of Steve Benz's strange behaviour towards the victim and of Emily's silent staring eyes.

"No, I don't think so," she lied.

Corrigan took a deep breath and leaned forward on the desk.

"The press hasn't got wind of this yet, but when they do, I'm expecting this place to be crawling with reporters. In particular, I think they'll be after you, Miss Blake."

"Me?...Oh." She suddenly realised how this

would look to the outside world. Mary Blake spends the weekend at a secluded country house with the woman who had replaced her, Melanie Shaw, who had now died from a blow to the head in the night. The British press would try, convict and sentence Mary by the end of the day.

"For that reason, I think it's best that the guests at the hall stay here for the time being until we can shed some more light on what's happened here."

Mary nodded. "And there will be a full investigation, will there?"

Corrigan looked at her curiously. "A young woman has died, Miss Blake."

"Yes, yes of course," Mary said hurriedly. "I was just wondering if you were treating the situation as suspicious or an accident."

Corrigan returned her gaze with interest. Mary felt as though she was wilting under it, as though he could read the guilt in her eyes.

"Is there something you'd like to tell me about the night that Miss Shaw died?"

Mary thought about the hushed conversation between her friends and about her own indiscretion with the laxative pills and looked him straight in the eye.

"Nothing at all," she said, her chin held high.

"Well, if anything should suddenly occur to you,"

he paused, as though he was convinced something had already occurred to her but was giving her the chance to say so, "please feel free to come and see me."

"Of course," Mary said stiffly, rising and leaving the room slowly, fighting the urge to run.

The rest of the group turned to her as she arrived back in the sitting room.

"They want us to all stay here a while, they think the press is going to turn up any minute."

"I should bloody well hope so," Flintock grumbled, looking at his phone. "I called them twenty minutes ago."

"You did what?!" Freddie Hale asked, incredulous.

"Look, I know this is a tragic time and all that," Flintock said, sounding like he had heard of the concept of grief, but didn't really believe in it. "But we've got to think of the future Freddie, that's what you pay me for, isn't it? To make the tough calls when they're needed?"

"And what on earth has that got to do with you calling the press in like vultures to pick over Melanie?!" Freddie raged, jumping up from the sofa and looming over his rotund agent.

"It's good publicity!" Flintock cried, jumping up

as well. "You're the grieving boyfriend now, we can use that!"

Freddie swung his fist violently at his agent, catching him on the nose and sending him sprawling back across the sofa, before turning and storming towards the French doors which led out onto the garden and wrenching them open. He marched away across the grounds without looking back.

"Let me get you a tissue," Emily said, pulling a packet from her pocket and leaning across to hand it to Flintock who was holding his nose and gasping with a shocked expression.

"He bloody hit me!" Flintock said, as the tissue that he had pressed against his nose turned crimson.

"You deserved it," Mary said. "He's upset and all you can do is see the marketing opportunity."

"That's what he pays me for!" Flintock said, waving his arms in exasperation. "Anyway, it's not as though he's lost the love of his life or anything, he wouldn't have even bloody known her if it wasn't for me."

"What do you mean?"

Flintock sighed. "Freddie and Melanie weren't really together, I made the whole thing happen for exposure. I met Melanie about six months ago at a club in London and I clocked her number straight away. The only thing she was ever interested in was furthering her own career and she didn't care who she stepped on to get there."

"That's a bit rich coming from you," Mary countered.

"I didn't say I was any different, did I?" he snapped. "No, I'd have bloody loved to have her as a client, she has... had, what it takes to get to the top in this business. She wouldn't have it though. She always wanted to do her own thing and get her own way. So, I worked out how I could use her anyway. I suggested that we could create a fake relationship between her and Freddie that would get the papers frothing at the mouth, and it worked." He grinned, still dabbing at his nose. "It's early days, we've just been feeding them little rumours, being pictured together and that kind of thing, but the two have them have never been more popular." He turned to Mary and laughed. "I reckon that might have been why she got your job you know."

Mary's teeth clenched involuntarily.

"So, they weren't really together?" Steve Benz who had been watching all of this with his usual quiet countenance.

Mary noticed Emily's eyes flash towards him.

"Of course not!" Flintock laughed. "But Melanie was a clever little sod and she was trying to fill Freddie's head with all sorts of nonsense."

"Like what?" Pea asked.

"Oh, you know, saying he'd be better off taking a leaf out of her book and managing things himself."

"Getting rid of you, you mean?" Mary said with an accusatory tone.

"He wasn't taking any notice of her of course," Flintock added hastily. "He's a clever boy is Freddie, he knows what's best for him. That Melanie could be poison though."

"Sounds like you might have had a pretty good reason for getting Melanie out of the way?" Mary immediately regretted her words, which were born from annoyance at this vile man. She felt the eyes of the room swivel to her, and then to Flintock.

"Don't be crazy," Flintock said, breaking the silence. "This had nothing to do with me! Anyway, she was locked in her room, wasn't she?"

"The window was open," Emily added quietly.

"And you think I climbed up there and smashed her over the head?" Flintock laughed. "I can barely make it up the stairs, love."

"I thought Melanie had fallen and hit her head?" Steve asked, looking at Mary questioningly.

"She might have done, I was just saying." Mary got up from the sofa and walked over to the French windows.

What a bloody mess this was! Soon the police

would find traces of those pills in Melanie's system and then they would conduct a search and she would...

Her train of thought derailed for a moment as she realised with a jolt that it wouldn't be her that the police suspected, it would be Dot. She was the one with the pills in her handbag. She was also the best friend of someone whose whole career had been thrown in the gutter while being replaced by the victim.

She couldn't do that to Dot. She was going to have to confess to slipping Melanie the pills before the police found them in her system, but that wouldn't be for a while yet, surely?

In the meantime, she would find out as much as she could about how Melanie had died. Hopefully, she would discover that the pills had been nothing to do with it.

"I'm just going to check on Freddie," she said over her shoulder, leaving through the French doors before anyone could protest or ask to join her.

CHAPTER TEN

The air was brisk, but not too cold. The sun's rays that lit up the grounds before her were strong enough to keep the chill at bay. She scanned the area in front of her for any sign of the actor, but he was nowhere to be seen. At the bottom of the gently sloping grass in front of her was the lake and beside it, the stone folly. If he had headed anywhere, it would almost certainly be there. She moved towards it, trying to ignore the many memories that were fighting for attention in her mind.

The folly had been another favourite spot of hers and Pea's when they had been younger. They had so often gone there, hidden from the eyes of the house behind them and made little paper boats that they would sail across the water.

The folly was a small, square building containing

a single, stone bench that overlooked the lake before it. It was a peaceful and tranquil space where they had huddled eating chocolate sneaked from the kitchen and watch the geese swim by.

The lake was much as she remembered it, with reed beds dotted along its banks, a few groups of lily pads floating on its surface, and the geese who honked bitterly at each other as they splashed in the water on the far side.

She wondered momentarily how long geese lived, and if any of these were ones she had seen as goslings many years ago.

As the narrow, gravel path she was following rounded the folly she saw Freddie Hale laying across the stone bench, staring up at the ceiling.

"You ok, Freddie?" she said, her voice echoing around the hard surface of the structure.

"Oh, bloody marvellous," he replied bitterly. He sighed and swung his legs down so that Mary could sit next to him.

"I know what she was like," he said quietly. "I'm not an idiot. Melanie had a lot of issues. She used to take them out on everyone else, but I think really she was a bit damaged herself."

"Aren't we all," Mary said sighing.

"She really did think you were great, you know.

She was excited about taking over your character and trying to do it justice."

Mary smiled and nodded at him, but this version of how Melanie felt about her didn't tally in her mind with the barbed tongue and sarcastic manner she had encountered in the late actress.

Suddenly she saw in his face the reason his version of Melanie was so distorted.

"You loved her, didn't you?"

He looked away across the lake. "Does that surprise you?"

"It does, actually," Mary answered. "Flintock has just been telling everyone how he put you two together for the publicity."

Freddie's gaze snapped back to her, his face flaring in anger. "Bloody Dave! He shouldn't have said that."

"Is it true?"

"Yes," he answered after a moment's pause. "He set it up. I hadn't even met her until we went out to a club together so that Dave could tip off the press."

"But it changed for you?"

"For both of us," he answered quickly. "We were both from the same world, we just clicked."

"And what did Flintock make of that?"

"He didn't care, all he's ever worried about is

getting people talking about me and making sure the press is following my every bloody move. This is all his fault, you know. If he could have just left us alone."

"I gather Melanie wasn't too fond of Flintock?"

Freddie laughed, shaking his head. "She thought he was a worm, and she's right. She wanted me to ditch him and sort out my own career."

"Which is what she did?"

"Yes," he said, a faraway look in his eye. "Melanie was very determined that the only person she could ever rely on was herself."

Mary sensed that there was frustration there. Had Melanie not allowed Freddie to be as close as he wanted them to be? He said she had felt the same way about him, but she had been cold enough to him last night and had refused to share a room with him.

There was something else though. Freddie didn't seem himself. It was though the words he was saying were playing from a tape, he was on auto-pilot. Melanie's death appeared to have broken him somehow.

"I should have gone with her last night," Freddie continued, "made sure she was ok."

"From what I saw, she didn't want you to," Mary said.

"No, as I said, she always thought she could

handle everything herself. She was ill though and I should have gone with her."

"I'd better get back," Mary said standing, keen to avoid revisiting Melanie's mysterious illness. "It's freezing out here. Why don't you come back with me?"

Freddie nodded and rose before following her out of the stone folly with a solemn expression.

"Does she have any family?" she asked as they followed the path back to the house.

"I don't think so, she never really talked about it but I got the impression her mother had died when she was young and her dad left the scene ages ago."

Mary felt a wave of sadness wash over her. Melanie Shaw might have been a spiteful young woman, but maybe she had good reason to be.

"I just wish she'd let me in last night," Freddie moaned.

"She was probably already unconscious by then," Mary said soothingly.

"No, she answered me."

Mary turned to him in surprise.

"Melanie answered you after I had seen you last night?"

"Yes, she told me she was fine and just wanted to be on her own. I should have forced her to let me in."

"And how did she sound?"

"I don't know," he shrugged, looking at Mary curiously. "It was through the door, she just told me to go away."

"That was late," Mary said thoughtfully. "She must have fallen between around two and eight or so in the morning."

"How do you know it must have been before eight?"

"Well, we found her at, what? Nine? And the blood had dried quite a lot, so I was giving it an hour or so."

They had reached the French doors to the sitting room and Freddie paused as his hand landed on the handle. He looked at Mary with something akin to disgust at her discussing Melanie's blood in such a matter-of-fact way. "I think I need to go and have a lie-down," he said gruffly, before entering the room and striding across it, ignoring the calls of Dave Flintock, whose nose seemed to have fully recovered.

"What did he say?" Flintock asked Mary as she came through the doors and into the room.

"Nothing, he's just upset. He's lost someone he was close to."

Flintock gave a mocking laugh and shook his head as he looked back at his phone.

"He needs to pull himself together, I've got people queueing up to interview him already."

"Alright?" Dot said as Mary joined her and Pea over in the corner of the room by the piano.

"Fine," Mary said looking around at the TV that Steve Benz and Emily Hanchurch were watching from the sofa.

"The press is already here," Mary said, nodding to the screen where news crews were standing outside the familiar gates of Blancham Hall, while a rolling ticker tape ran across the bottom of the screen, which declared Melanie Shaw dead.

"They are," Pea answered. "Bloody hundreds of them out at the gates already. The police are keeping them back for now, but you know what they're like. Um, Mary,"

His change in tone brought Mary's gaze away from the set and back to him.

"What is it?"

Pea turned to Dot looking sheepish.

"They know you're staying here somehow, Mary, and they're putting two and two together," Dot said flatly.

"What do you mean putting two and two together?" Mary asked. She already knew exactly what they meant, but for some reason, she was enjoying them squirm over telling her. Maybe some slight payback for keeping secrets.

"They think you might have bumped her off," Pea said.

"Oh, right," Mary said, looking at the both of them.

"You don't seem very shocked," Pea laughed. "You didn't actually do it, did you?!" He laughed again, but then stopped as he saw Mary's face.

"Bloody hell Mary, you didn't, did you?!"

"Of course I didn't!" Mary hissed, looking around to see if the others had overheard their conversation, but all were engrossed in the news report.

"What is it, Mary?" Dot asked.

Mary looked around again before leaning in closer to the two of them. "I may have done something a little bit silly last night."

"You gave Melanie my pills, didn't you?" Dot said.

"What?!" Pea said loudly, making the rest of the room look up.

Mary shushed him urgently and waited for the others in the room to turn back to the TV before continuing.

"How did you know?" she asked Dot.

"Oh, it wasn't hard to figure out," Dot said sighing. "I noticed there were four pills missing when I went to take them this morning and then I thought about Melanie rushing off to bed and you getting her a drink just before."

"Will someone tell me what's going on?!" Pea said excitedly.

"I took some of Dot's pills and slipped them to Melanie."

"Bloody hell!" Pea said, eyes wide in his thin face. "What were they?"

"They were laxatives, if you must know," Dot said primly, adjusting the plum-coloured cardigan she wore.

"Oh, right," Pea said, looking embarrassed and puzzled at the same time.

"I'm sure it's nothing to do with what happened," Mary said, her voice sounding more hopeful than anything, even to her own ears.

"Well, how could it?" Pea asked. "I mean, she might be stuck on the toilet for a little bit, but they're hardly likely to cause her head to get bashed in, are they?"

"They could have interacted with some other medication," Dot said, looking Mary in the eye.

"YOU DON'T REALLY THINK..." Mary began but was cut off by her friend.

"No, I'm sure it was nothing to do with it." Dot said firmly. "But the police might not see it like that."

"The police? But they don't think I had anything to do with it surely?"

"Oh, come on, Mary," Dot tutted. "Of course they do, you'll be their prime suspect, and that's before they discover you tried to poison her."

"I didn't try and poison her!"

"Do you think that's what the press will say?"

Mary opened her mouth but closed it again without saying anything. If she didn't know better, she could have sworn that Dot was enjoying this.

"This is good news in a way through," Pea said. "I mean, Flintock might be an insufferable sod, but he's right, this will be great for your career."

"Pea!" Mary said shocked. "I wasn't a big fan of Melanie, but bloody hell."

"Sorry," he said, looking again at Dot. "But it's important you get back on track career-wise."

Mary looked at Dot who was decidedly not returning Pea's furtive glances.

"Why is it?" she asked coldly.

"Sorry, why is what?"

"Why is it so important I get my career back on track."

"Um," Pea said before Dot cut across him.

"We're just worried about you Mary, we're your friends," she said as though the matter was closed.

Mary turned away from them in annoyance. There was something going on between the two of them, they were having secret meetings and seemed convinced that she was about to fall apart unless they got her back into work.

Well, she was doing just fine, thank you very much. Yes, she had probably wallowed for a bit and drunk too many G&Ts, and, yes, she had slipped some laxatives into Melanie's drink, but who wouldn't have done the same in her situation?

She realised that Dot and Pea were talking, discussing how they could get everyone some food, but she wasn't really paying attention.

Instead, she was watching the three people sitting on the sofa across the room. Flintock was still glued to his phone, only occasionally looking up at the TV screen while his stubby fingers whirled away on his keypad. Mary shuddered to think how he was using the situation to further Freddie Hale's career.

The two of more interest to her though were Steve Benz and Emily Hanchurch. Steve was slumped, his head leaning on his right hand as he stared listlessly at the screen. His eyes were puffy and red, his skin pale. Mary had the impression that he wasn't so much watching the screen in front of him as just gazing at nothing.

Emily Hanchurch, on the other hand, was much more alert. She was perched forward on the edge of the sofa like a very tall bird. Looking intently at the screen, but every few moments, turning to glance at Steve next to her.

They were next to each other on the sofa, but Mary noticed that the distance between them seemed slightly wider than was natural. She wondered if they were maybe regretting their late-night tryst.

There was something else about Steve that unsettled her. His eyes looked more than just in a daze—they looked switched off, as though he had checked out completely.

"Speak of the devil," Pea said, pulling his phone from his pocket and moving away from them.

"Who?" Mary said spinning around.

"Hetty, I'd imagine, weren't you listening?" Dot said, looking at her curiously.

"She was supposed to be up here making breakfast but hasn't turned up and it's past lunch now. Is everything alright?"

"Well, that's a stupid bloody question, isn't it?!" Mary said, folding her arms. "Of course I'm not alright! Melanie's been murdered, half the world seems to think I'm the prime suspect and, to top it all, I actually might be once they find out I slipped her some pills just a few hours before she bashed her head open."

She had poured this out in a low, angry whisper, but now vented, her shoulders slumped as her eyes filled with tears.

"Bloody hell, Dot," she said, her voice thick with emotion. "What if she fell because of the pills. What if it was all my fault?"

"There's no point in thinking like that until we know more," Dot said firmly, "and whatever you do don't say anything of the kind to the police."

"They're going to find out eventually," Mary said gloomily.

"They will, but before they do, I'm going to tell them that I gave them to her."

Mary looked up at her friend in shock.

"What are you talking about?!"

"I'm going to tell them that the pills were mine and at some point in the night I thought I'd play a joke on Melanie and slipped her some."

"Don't be ridiculous. I'm not a child, Dot, I can look after myself."

"Believe me, this is best," Dot said.

Before Mary could protest further, Pea joined them again. "Hetty's down at the front gate, apparently it's chaos down there and the officers won't let her through without say-so from the big boss up here at the house. I'll go and ask this Inspector Corrigan if she can come up. We do have to eat, after all."

He grinned at them both and turned away, heading back towards the hallway.

Pea was always uneasy whenever anyone was arguing around him and tended to talk incessantly to prevent the argument from continuing until he found an excuse to get away. Mary sensed that that was what had just happened here.

She stared across at the TV, which was still droning on in the background. The rolling news station it was set to had moved to back to its usual cycle of daily events. But the gates, which were just a few hundred yards from where they were standing, still reappeared periodically and scrolling across a yellow banner at the bottom of the screen in-between was the news of Melanie's death. Seeing it on the screen suddenly made everything seem very real.

"I'm not going to let you take the blame for something I've done, Dot," Mary said firmly.

"A fat lot of good your sense of integrity will do when the press is all over you because you're the prime suspect in a murder case. Who knows what they'll dig up?"

"What's that supposed to mean?" she said turning to her.

Dot sighed and rolled her eyes to the ceiling. "Look, I think we need to talk,"

"You mean about how you and Pea seem to be having private little chats about me late at night?" Mary said, suddenly feeling a flash of anger pass through her. From Dot's face, Mary knew her words had hit home. Her friend's eyes widened and her skin paled before her cheeks flushed a deep red.

"Don't worry, I didn't tell the police that you were up at all hours having secret meetings."

"We've only ever had your best interests in mind," Dot said in a sad, resigned voice.

There was something in the way she had said it that rocked Mary. How long had this been going on? How long had they been talking about her, plotting between them about how to manage her? Was she really that crazy?

"For God's sake!" a voice screamed from behind her. She spun around to see Steve Benz, his face contorted in fury as he loomed over Emily Hanchurch on the sofa.

"A woman has died!" he continued. "Show some respect and bloody well leave me alone!" He stormed from the room leaving Flintock cackling in his armchair.

"I thought it was the actors that were supposed to be the drama queens?" he said laughing. "The bloody producers are just as bad!"

"Oh, be quiet, Flintock," Mary said, moving across the room to Emily who was sitting wide-eyed with tears streaming down her face.

"Come on," Mary said, holding her hand out to her. "Why don't we go for a little walk, a bit of fresh air will make you feel better."

Emily nodded and got up as though in a daze. Mary shot a look at Dot that she hoped conveyed a clear message not to follow her and led Emily out into the hall where she grabbed their coats from the stand and headed out through the main entrance.

"We're just going for a walk around the house," she said to the young officer who was standing there. His mouth opened, about to protest, when he saw the tears that were still rolling down Emily's pale cheeks and instead just nodded and moved aside.

The power of a crying woman, Mary thought as she turned her companion right along the path that ran in front of the house. She held Emily's arm, which even through the thickness of the coat she could feel was as thin and hard as bone. Added to her pale complexion, Mary rather cruelly thought of her as almost skeletal in appearance. Despite this, she was a good-looking woman. Her high cheekbones and striking green eyes were assurance of that.

"So, are you and Steve are an item then?" Mary said, always favouring bluntness over delicacy.

"I, I'm not sure any more," Emily stammered, her voice thin and punctuated by sobs. "I thought we were, but..."

"I saw you going into his room last night, was that the first time you'd been together?"

"Oh no, we've been seeing each other for a while now. We met at an on-set party through mutual friends a few months ago."

"Oh, right," Mary said, puzzled. "Sorry for saying, but you haven't seemed overly 'together' since you've been here?"

"Something's wrong with Steve," Emily blurted out, her bottom lip wobbling. "I don't know what it is, but he's been all strange since the day before we got here and he just won't talk to me. He's been pushing me away and then, well, today!"

"What about today?"

"Melanie dying has sent him completely crazy." She paused and wiped her eyes with her sleeve. "And now I'm starting to wonder if the reason he was being so cold to me was because Melanie was here."

"Surely you don't think there was anything going on between them?!" Mary said incredulously. Steve

Benz was in his mid-fifties, and not exactly a catch. There was no way she could see Melanie Shaw being interested in him in a million years.

"Steve is a successful producer, Melanie was probably fluttering her eyelashes at him to get her a part in a show or something. And then last night," she said shaking her head as though trying to shake the memories out.

"What happened last night?" Mary asked, stopping and halting Emily with a touch of her arm. They had rounded to the corner to the back of the house and on the far side, two officers were still combing the area for signs of an intruder.

"He was, just awful," Emily said speaking slowly and dramatically, her whole body shaking with either hurt or anger, Mary couldn't tell. "I went to his room, but he said it was all over and that he couldn't see me anymore. Just like that!"

"And did he say why?" Mary asked, stepping back slightly. Emily looked like a woman on the edge.

"He said his life was moving in another direction now and we didn't fit into that, whatever that means."

"Anyway," Emily said bitterly, "he told me to get out."

"And have you spoken about it this morning?"

"I was trying to when he began shouting at me, he's barely said a word all morning."

"Come on," Mary said taking her arm. "Let's head back, I'll try and talk to him for you."

"Oh, would you? Thank you," Emily said beaming, she squeezed Mary's arm as they turned around and made their way back to the house.

CHAPTER ELEVEN

"What's going on?" Mary said as she and Emily arrived back in the hallway of the house.

Dot, Pea, Dave and Freddie were all heading up the stairs in a line. Dot turned at the sound of her voice.

"Oh, Mary, I wondered where you were. I stuck my head out the front door, but there was no sign of you."

"We'd gone around the side of the house, what's happening?"

"The police are going to search all of our rooms, they want us there while they do it."

"Oh, right," Mary answered, following the group up the stairs in a daze, gripped with a sudden fear.

Once they searched the rooms, they would find Dot's laxatives. As soon as the post mortem revealed that they had been in Melanie's system, Dot would confess and the evidence would back her up. Mary needed to get ahead of this. She needed to talk to Inspector Corrigan now.

As they reached the landing and began to fan out towards each of their rooms, she saw the Inspector was standing outside hers, a female uniformed officer by his side.

Mary felt her breathing quicken.

Why was he waiting outside her room? All the others had a single police officer outside, but the man in charge had apparently decided that she was worthy of his special attention.

"Inspector," she greeted him curtly.

"Miss Blake," he replied, that slight smile that always seemed only moments from his lips appearing again. "I'm sorry for the intrusion, but I assure you this is necessary."

"It's quite alright," Mary said stiffly. "Actually, I need to tell you something."

She looked over her shoulder, but as Melanie's room had been the one next to hers and she was at the end, there was no one in earshot.

"Why don't we go into your room to talk?"

Corrigan said, his face now serious and business-like. "Constable Jones here can begin searching your room while we do so, if that's OK with you?"

"Fine," Mary said, before following them both through the door.

"Big room," Corrigan said looking around.

"They're all big rooms here," Mary said.

She moved to the small sofa under the right-hand window and decidedly took her seat in the middle, ensuring there was no room for Corrigan. Instead, he pulled the red, padded chair from in front of the dressing table and dragged it in front of her.

"OK," he said leaning forward with his elbows on his knees. "What do you want to tell me?"

Mary sighed and looked down at the worn carpet.

She was reminded of the time at school when she had hit Henry Chadworth with her hockey stick for grabbing at her breasts in the playground. Sitting before an unsympathetic headmaster, she had been defiant then. Righteous in the knowledge that she had done the right thing and that that boy had got exactly what he had deserved.

Now though? Now she felt small, awkward, and, most of all, guilty.

The uniformed officer, who had begun mooching

around the room as soon as they had entered, begun looking through the bedside drawers. Mary watched her as her mind tried to ignore her current situation by lingering in the past.

Henry Chadworth, she remembered, had gone on to be a politician.

"Last night, purely as a prank, I took some tablets from my friend's handbag and slipped them into Melanie Shaw's drink," she said in a rush of words that tumbled out of her mouth before she folded her arms and stared at the Inspector as though daring him to say the obvious.

"OK, thank you for telling me."

"Look, just because I wanted to give her a dodgy tummy for a while, doesn't mean I'd..." She paused and frowned, realising he had not accused her of murdering Melanie as she had thought he would.

"How many pills?" he asked, ignoring her outburst.

"Four," she answered, and then added quickly, "but I don't think that's enough to do anything really bad. I mean, the recommended dose is two tablets!"

She realised she sounded more hopeful and desperate than convincing and was relieved when she saw Corrigan give her a sympathetic look.

"I can't see how it could have anything to do with her injuries," he said softly. "But I have to say this doesn't help you to look any more innocent, Miss Blake."

Mary said nothing, sensing from the look in the Inspector's eye that he had more to say.

"Crime scene says there's no sign of any part of the furniture having been the cause of Miss Shaw's death," he said grimly. "We are now treating this as a murder."

"Bloody hell," Mary said, leaning back in her seat as puffed out her cheeks and exhaled in surprise.

"The only problem is," Corrigan continued, his eyes looking up to the ceiling. "We have no sign of a murder weapon, no clue how someone could have entered the room and then exited with a thick, solid door locked from the inside and a sheer wall outside the window."

His gaze returned to her suddenly, as though he had just realised how much he was sharing with her.

"Are you sure you didn't hear any sounds from next door last night? A bang? Scuffling? Anything at all?"

"Nothing," Mary said, still unwilling to report on her friend's nocturnal meeting, and then frowned.

"What is it?" Corrigan asked, his voice rising in sudden expectation.

"I've just remembered that I did hear a kind of

thump, and a sort of tapping noise just before it now I think of it,"

"A tapping, and a thump," Corrigan repeated slowly.

Mary felt she had disappointed him and to her own surprise, wanted to help some other way.

"What about the window?" she asked.

"What about it?" Corrigan answered. "I've already said, scaling that wall seems unlikely."

"No, I don't mean that," Mary continued. "I mean, what if someone threw something through it, like a rock or something. Or fired it."

"Like a catapult?" Corrigan smiled.

"Well," Mary huffed, slightly hurt at his amusement. "It's a possible answer, isn't it? That's more than you've got now."

"If something had been thrown through the window it would still be in the room," Corrigan said, the smile was gone now. "We didn't find anything. There's hardly anything in the whole room that could have hit her over the head and what there is we've tested and found no traces on it."

"Sir?" the police officer said from across the room. She was standing by the bed, holding a small piece of paper and staring at Mary strangely.

"Stay here please, Miss Blake," Corrigan said,

giving her a sharp look as he rose and moved across the room.

The officer held out the paper to him with a latex-gloved hand and his eyes scanned it before turning back to Mary.

"I'm afraid it looks like we have even more to discuss, Miss Blake," he said flatly.

CHAPTER TWELVE

"You could at least tell me what it says," Mary said haughtily. She was desperately trying to keep the rising terror at bay by channelling it into being bloody furious instead. The way they were acting had her worried. What on earth could they have found in here that would have them both looking at her as though she was some kind of mass murderer?!

"Or maybe that's your plan?" she said angrily. "It's probably just some scrap of paper that's been in here for years and you're just pretending that it's something to do with what happened to Melanie."

Corrigan had said nothing for at least two minutes since the uniformed officer had handed him the note. The constable had continued her search of the room while Corrigan had taken a seat back on the chair by the dresser and stared at Mary with a blank and unreadable expression.

Finally, the officer emerged for the bathroom and nodded at her superior.

"That's it, Sir, nothing else," she said before standing against the wall with her hands together in front of her, staring off into space.

"Miss Blake, this piece of paper," Corrigan said, holding up the small see-through plastic bag that contained it in front of him. "Says 'you are the killer!' in a printed font."

"What?!" Mary said sitting up in her chair wide-eyed.

"And bearing in mind it was found under your pillow, I have to wonder why or how it got there?"

"Well, how the hell am I supposed to know?!" Mary said, throwing her hands into the air exasperated. "You don't seriously think that Melanie took the time to get to a computer and write an incriminating note after I'd whacked her over the head, do you?"

Corrigan said nothing, but the corner of his mouth rose and his eyes took on a questioning quality.

"Oh, I didn't mean I'd actually bashed her over

the head! I'm just pointing out how ridiculous all of this is!"

"As ridiculous as a murder in a locked and inaccessible room?" Corrigan asked dryly.

Mary opened her mouth to answer, then closed it again as Corrigan got up and moved across the room to the window on the left-hand side. He opened it and leaned his head out for a moment before pulling back in, shutting it and returning to his chair.

"You know?" he said sighing. "The climb in through Melanie Shaw's window would be a lot less difficult if you were going across from yours rather than all the way from the ground up."

"You can't be serious?! I'm not some bloody spider-woman crawling all over the building!"

"I'm just presenting you with the current situation," Corrigan said. "A woman has been killed and right now, you look like the most likely candidate for the murder."

Mary swallowed, her throat suddenly dry. The full weight of Melanie's death being murder hit her, alongside the terror of being the prime suspect. All those shows where she had chased down the bad guy, her well-practised look of righteousness plastered across her face.

Now though, in real life and the other side of the questioning, it was horrible.

"Are you OK?" Corrigan asked, his head tilting on one side.

"Fine," Mary croaked. "What happens now?"

Corrigan took a deep breath, his deep brown eyes fixed on hers.

"Did you murder Melanie Shaw?"

The words hit Mary like a boot to the chest. She cleared her throat and returned the intensity of his stare.

"No, I did not."

He held her gaze for a moment in silence before nodding and rising from his chair.

"Thank you, Miss Blake, we'll talk again once I've checked about the other rooms." He left, closely followed by the officer.

Mary took a seat and tried to gather her thoughts. What on earth was she going to do?

Her head snapped up from the floor as she heard raised voices coming from the hallway and she sprang from the sofa and headed towards it.

In the corridor, the rest of the guests were lined up outside their respective doors. That is, apart from Freddie Hale, whose arms were being held back by two officers as red face contorted in anger and frustration.

"What is it, Benz? What did they find?!"

Steve Benz was standing outside his door with a pale, sorrowful expression, his eyes downwards and his shoulders hunched. Inspector Corrigan was standing next to him, looking into a small bag next to a uniformed officer. He looked up and gestured to the officer who led Steve Benz back into his room.

"Can you please escort everyone else downstairs?" Corrigan said to the officers who began rounding up the guests with Freddie Hale in front still swearing and mumbling under his breath as he shook off the officers now loosened grip.

Once back in the living room, Freddie made his way straight for the small bar in the corner and poured himself a whiskey that Mary considered stiff even by her standards. Dave Flintock moved across to his client and laid a hand on his back, which was quickly brushed off by Freddie, who stormed across to the windows with his drink. Flintock shrugged and began looking through the bottles on offer at the bar.

Emily Hanchurch had returned to the sofa and was sitting there in pale-faced silence, staring at the blank television screen without turning it on again.

"What's going on?" Mary asked as Dot and Pea appeared either side of her by the door.

"They found some sort of note in Steve Benz's room." Dot answered.

Mary frowned. "In Steve's room?"

"Yes," Dot continued, eyeing Mary suspiciously. "And I noticed the Inspector had something from your room as well?"

"What?!" Pea said, his eyes widening.

Mary sighed as she looked between them. "It was a note which apparently says that I'm Melanie's killer."

"Bloody hell!" Pea gasped. "Someone thinks you killed her? And they snuck into your room to leave a note?!"

"Where was it?" Dot asked.

"Under my pillow."

"And did you see it?"

"Not really, he just flashed it at me. It was printed though, which doesn't make any... wait!"

Mary pushed through the two of them and ran for the door, bursting through into the hall and barging straight into the officer who had been waiting on the other side.

"I'm sorry!" she called to him as she raced up the stairs, ignoring his shouts for her to stop from behind.

The door to Steve Benz's room was open and she pushed it wide and stepped into the room.

"It was from the game!" she boomed triumphantly.

Corrigan jumped up from the chair he had been

sitting in, facing Benz, and moved quickly towards her.

"Out, now," he said firmly, taking her arm and sending her spinning back into the corridor."

"This is a murder investigation," he growled as they spilt out into the corridor. "You can't just walk into a room where I am interrogating a suspect and start talking about some game or other!"

Mary recoiled from his ferocity, taken aback but his change in manner. His soft eyes had hardened and narrowed, his mouth tightened and his jaw set. He seethed like a bear who had just been woken from hibernation early.

"Wait," he said suddenly looking puzzled. "Why were you talking about, a game?"

The anger had vanished as quickly as it had come and Mary straightened her back and lifted her chin.

"Well, if you'd just listened rather than leaping about and manhandling me," she said, giving him an accusing look. She was surprised to see his cheeks redden and feeling uncomfortable herself, moved on quickly.

"Anyway, I've realised that the note you found in my room wasn't really a note."

"What do you mean?"

"It was printed, right? Well, who could have the

time to print it between me apparently murdering Melanie and you searching the rooms? And in any case, if someone had left it for me they would put it somewhere more obvious than under my pillow."

"You could have hidden it there?" Corrigan said, his eyes twinkling with amusement again.

"I think you can give me a little more credit than that Inspector. I would have burnt it or flushed it down the toilet or something, not kept it under my pillow like it was a love note from an admirer."

His eyes darted away for hers for an instant and he shuffled on his feet before looking back at her.

"So, what exactly has this got to do with a game?"

"The murder mystery game," Mary said triumphantly. "I was the murderer in the game, I bet the text is from the scripts we were all given."

"And have you gone to find your script for last night to check?" Corrigan asked, raising an eyebrow.

"Oh, no." Mary folded her arms, annoyed that she hadn't thought of this before running upstairs and causing a scene. "But I can go and ask Pea where they are!" she said, already turning to go.

Something tugged at her mind and she stopped and turned back to where Corrigan was waiting with an expectant expression.

"Hold on," she said slowly. "Even if it was from

the script, how on earth did that part get torn out and left under my pillow?"

Corrigan smiled and nodded. "Now you're asking the right questions," he said. "And while you're thinking along those lines, you might want to think about who underlined the sentence saying you were the killer in red biro."

CHAPTER THIRTEEN

"The scripts?" Pea said in confusion.

Mary, Inspector Corrigan and the uniformed officer that had searched Mary's room were standing in front of him.

"Yes, where did you put them after we'd finished last night?"

"Um, in the library, I think. Why?"

"Come on," Mary said to Corrigan, turning and heading back to the hallway. "The rest of the guests can remain here," he said to a constable by the door, and the officer gently led Dot and Pea back into the living room.

As they had descended the stairs in search of the scripts from the murder mystery evening, Mary's mood had swung violently.

Her initial feelings of fear and concern at being a suspect in the murder of Melanie Shaw had given way to furious anger. Somebody else had murdered Melanie, and not only that, they had then tried to implicate her. There was no other explanation for the small scrap of the script that claimed her to be the killer finding its way under her pillow. The fact that someone had taken the time to underline the fact by hand just seemed like a further insult.

What had really sent her into a determined rage though, was the knowledge that it had to have been someone in the house. No intruder would have known about the murder mystery scripts, nor would they have known, in the dead of night, that Mary's room was next to Melanie's and would provide a perfect prime suspect.

She opened the library door and stepped into the large space. Tall windows ran along the right-hand wall, spilling light across the threadbare carpet, but not reaching the tall shelves of books that lined the other three walls. She headed for a round, leather-topped table which was positioned next to an armchair under the nearest window, its surface covered with a stack of paper.

"Don't touch anything!" Corrigan called from behind and she pulled back from the table as though flames had licked her fingers. He moved alongside her in the small space and peered down at the scripts. "I'll get crime scene to go over them," he said grimly. "But it looks like your theory was right."

He pointed to the far corner of the pile where a script lay upside down with its final page torn across the bottom.

He turned to her and folded his arms, a frown deepening across his brow.

"I am concerned, Miss Blake, that somebody is attempting to frame you for the murder of Melanie Shaw."

"Well, that makes two of us," Mary said, folding her arms to match his.

He looked down at her from the two or three inches in height he had over her. His broad shoulders seemed to fill Mary's vision in what felt like the suddenly small space of the study. She felt a prickle of heat rising up the back of her neck.

He glanced towards the door back into the hall which was still half open, the back of the uniformed officer outside just visible, before returning his gaze to her, his voice low.

"It doesn't make sense that someone planted that scrap of script under your pillow to implicate you. Why wouldn't they just come to us and tell us what they know? Having said that, you would be the obvious suspect, and a desperate mind doesn't make rational decisions. The real problem is that that means that the killer is almost certainly in the house. One of the people staying here last night killed Melanie Shaw, and now they want you to pay for it."

"We need to question them all again," Mary said firmly.

"We?" Corrigan smiled.

"Look, I'm the one who's being framed here, I think I have a right to find out who."

He took a deep breath and to Mary's surprise, nodded.

"You do," he said softly. "And I will find out for you. In the meantime, I think you're best served staying with the other guests. I need you to let me know anything that might help us, anything you hear from the others, anything that might have some bearing on the case."

"You mean work from the inside for you?" Mary caught the excitement in her own voice too late and saw his expression grow hard and stern.

"No, I just mean that if you hear anything, it would be in your best interests to inform me immediately. If someone took the time to tear this section of the script out and place it under your pillow after they had committed the murder, then who knows what they might do next to frame you?"

Mary bit her lip and looked to her right at the scripts strewn across the desk and thought about the secret meeting of her two friends Dot and Pea.

"Is there anything else you want to tell me?" Corrigan asked, perhaps sensing that something was on her mind.

"No," she said firmly, turning back to him.

"Right, well I'll have a uniform with the group at all times from now on, and outside your door tonight if it comes to that."

"We're staying here tonight?"

"If I bring all of you lot back to the station with half the country's press on my tail the Chief Inspector will have me on a desk filling out forms for the rest of my life. We've decided to keep you all here until we can get further along in the case. Come on," he nodded towards the door and Mary moved towards it and then stopped.

"What did you find in Steve Benz's room?"

"Don't worry about that," Corrigan said, with the look of exacerbation.

"But it was a note wasn't it? Like the one in my room?"

"No, not like the one in your room," he said flatly.

"Please escort Miss Blake into the living room, Constable."

The officer nodded and led a scowling Mary across the hall and back into the large room where the rest of the guests were still present.

Freddie Hale was still slumped in an armchair he had dragged in front of the French doors to the grounds, although not visible, she spotted a renewed and large glass of whiskey in his hand, which stuck out to one side. Emily Hanchurch and Dave Flintock were still sitting on the sofas in front of the television, though Flintock's attention was firmly on his phone, which he hammered away at with both thumbs.

Dot and Pea rushed over to her from the bar where they had been sitting on stools.

"Well? What's going on?" Pea asked. His narrow, pinched face was alive with excitement. Dot's square jaw and delicate features, however, remained impassive.

"I need to talk to you both," Mary said quietly. "Let's go back to the bar, I could do with a drink."

The three of them headed back, Mary positioning herself on the far side in order to give herself a view of the room where she could spot any of the others approaching. Emily was watching them, as though she wanted to ask if Mary had any news on

Steve Benz's fate, but seemed too timid to make an approach.

She watched as Dot made her a gin and tonic in the same methodical, mechanical and careful way that she did everything. Pea watched her from across the bar expectantly, like a puppy waiting for his owner to throw him a treat.

How could these two be keeping things from her? And if they could have secrets like that, could one of them have decided to frame her? But what possible motive would they have? She was being silly. Rattled by the events of the weekend she was starting to see things that weren't there. She just needed to ask them outright.

"What's going on between you two?" she asked as Dot slid her drink.

She watched their reactions. Pea jolted upright, his mouth opening in surprise as he turned to Dot for assistance.

"What do you mean?" Dot asked, her chin rising defiantly.

"I mean, what were you two meeting about secretly on the night Melanie was killed?"

"Oh, bloody hell," Pea said in a hoarse voice.

"Did you tell the police?" Dot asked quickly.

"No, I did not bloody well tell the police," Mary snapped. "That's not really the important question here though is it, Dot? The question is, what are you two not telling me?"

Dot sighed and looked down at the drink in front of her. Mary turned to Pea.

"It's Dad," he said softly.

"What's happened?" Mary said sitting upright. "Is he ok?"

"He's fine," Pea answered, "well, no change."

Mary nodded and relaxed again.

"Then what about him?"

"I went to visit him last week and there was a short time when he appeared lucid."

Mary felt a wave of guilt. She hadn't visited in months, she couldn't bear to see her father changed, diminished. The bright intellect and humour dulled and fogged by confusion and fear.

"He said there's something that we should know, something about mum."

Mary frowned in confusion.

"Mum? What do you mean?"

"Look, Mary. I didn't want to get into all this while you were..." He hesitated and glanced across to Dot.

"He means while you were wallowing, Mary," Dot said in her no-nonsense manner.

"Don't let him drag you into his protective older

brother act," Mary snapped. "Tell me what's going on."

"I was talking to dad about the problems on the estate," Pea said with a sigh. "The repair costs just keep spiralling and there just seems to always be something new that needs fixing or updating,"

"Yes, I know," Mary said impatiently, "can we just skip to the part about mum?"

"Well, I was telling him all this and he suddenly looked me straight in the eye and said I needed to get to the family secret."

"What does that mean?"

"I've no idea, I asked him and he just laughed and said, 'Don't you remember? Not all stories are fiction you know.' And then he said that mum was a cunning devil, and that she'd made sure it had stayed safe for us."

"And he didn't say what this family secret might be?"

"No, he just said it would solve all our problems." He shrugged. "And then something about the answers being here at Blancham." He reached out and took her hands in his. "Who knows how much of this is in reality and how much is in his fantasy world, but I haven't seen him as clear on anything for a long time Mary."

"So, whatever this secret is, mum knew about it,"

Mary said, thinking hard. "But what on earth could it be that could solve all of our problems?"

Pea and Dot both looked at their drinks simultaneously.

Mary eyed them suspiciously. Why hadn't they told her this? So, her father had said something about a family secret, in his condition that could mean anything.

"What is it you two aren't telling me?" She said flatly.

Pea looked up at her, glanced at Dot and then sighed. "Dad said something about a baby."

"A baby?"

Pea nodded and shrugged.

"What baby?"

"We don't know, Mary, it could be anything."

"A family secret..." Mary said in a whisper. The three of them fell silent as they all contemplated the obvious conclusion. Could there really be a 'secret baby' in the family?

"Maybe it's a secret Hollywood contract for you, Mary," Pea grinned sheepishly, trying to break the ice. She pulled one hand away from hers and slapped him on the wrist.

"Less of the cheek and more thinking about how we could find out who," she hesitated, "or what this is all about," she said, watching Pea rub the back of his wrist, wincing in pain.

"How can we find out?" Mary asked. "There must be someone else who knows about it,"

"I've looked into it a bit. Most of the people from mum and dad's circle are dead."

Mary looked down at the wooden surface of the bar in front of her. Soon her father would be gone too. At 84, he had lived a full life, but the reality was that it had ended ten years earlier when her mother had died. He had become quiet, introverted. Hiding away in his study for days on end and shutting out the world until, eventually, his mind had begun to decay along with his spirit.

Mary frowned as something jarred her from these nostalgic thoughts.

"Wait, what was that you were saying about a 'fool's bum' or something? The other night when you were having your secret meeting."

Pea sighed. "Dad said something about the answer being here at Blancham and then he said you'd find it under a fool's bottom."

There was a fraction of silence before Mary burst into laughter. Finding her father's words even more ridiculous as they jolted her from her sombre, questioning mood.

"Yes, he might have regressed a bit by that point,"

Pea said smiling. "Look, Mary. When this is all over, we'll investigate this together, get to the bottom of it, ok?" He reached out and took her hand. "It's probably nothing."

"OK," Mary said, squeezing his hand in return, "but I'm not someone that you both need to protect," she said to both of them sternly.

They both nodded, Pea with a sheepish grin and Dot with pursed lips which suggested she wasn't sure she believed her.

Mary knew now why they hadn't told her. They had seen her wallowing in her flat, soaked in gin and thought she was in a delicate mental state. Probably correctly, Mary thought. For the first time she realised how much the loss of the show had affected her and shuddered.

"Mary," Dave Flintock said in a voice like treacle.

He had risen from the sofa and was moving towards them with his palms facing outwards, a smile on his piggy face. "You and I should talk, we could use this publicity. The press is all over you as some crazed revenge killer, it's just perfect! There's never been a better time to get your career back on track!"

Mary felt the anger and frustration from today rise inside her. This small, toad-like man didn't care about Melanie, he didn't care about anyone. He only cared about himself.

Melanie's senseless death, her father, sitting in a room with his once-fine mind turned to mush, a baby mentioned and a family secret, and here was Flintock trying to take advantage, trying to use her.

She got up from her stool, moved around the bar and punched him square on the nose.

CHAPTER FOURTEEN

Mary was standing in the small bathroom and staring at herself in the mirror. She felt and looked old. Dark rings circled her eyes, which contrasted against her pale and washed-out skin. Her dark hair, which was normally styled up at the back allowing loose ringlets down either side of her face, was currently just a straight, hanging mess.

She looked down at her knuckles as the cold water from the tap poured over them. She had broken the skin on one, but it was the dull ache that throbbed throughout her entire hand that hurt more. It would be bruised for a while. Flintock's head must be made of granite, which, now she thought of it, could explain a few things. Having already been hit once that day, his nose had exploded in crimson. Pea was almost certainly going to have to get new carpets in the living room.

There had been some kerfuffle as the uniformed officer had run across from the doorway to restrain her, but then couldn't quite bring himself to do it when she was swearing like a trooper and clutching her fist.

She had beat a hasty retreat to the small bathroom of the main hall and was now considering staying there for the rest of the day. She wasn't sure she could face that room again, with those petulant and self-absorbed people along with her two friends who, even if it was because they were concerned about her wellbeing, had lied to her.

Mary sighed and closed her eyes. With her right big toe still aching like crazy from stubbing it on the stone earlier, she was fast becoming the walking wounded.

She blinked in surprise as she realised that she was crying. Crying for Melanie, crying because of the betrayal, and even crying for the sister she was sure she had lost.

She stifled her sobs as she heard a voice from outside.

"Yes, sir, I realise that," the voice said, and she recognised the dulcet tones of Inspector Corrigan.

"The press is being kept at the main gate for now, but we've already caught two trying to sneak onto the grounds. We're a bit stretched for men if we're being honest, Sir."

Mary crept over to the door that separated her from the hall and gently pressed her ear against it.

"Yes, I am considering her as a suspect, Sir," Corrigan continued, causing Mary to catch her breath. "We found the note I told you about in her room implying she was the killer, but we think it may have been planted there in order to throw suspicion on her."

Mary could hear the voice on the other end of the line barking but couldn't make out any words.

"Of course, Sir, but I also realise the sensitivity of the case," Corrigan continued. "Believe me, she's our number one suspect, but we wouldn't want to go too far down that road in the glare of the public eye unless we're sure."

Mary felt a rush of gratitude for Corrigan. She had already had the impression that he didn't really see her as a realistic suspect, but now it sounded as though he was trying to not expose her to the madness of the press as well. Though from watching the TV earlier, she suspected it was too late.

"We did find a note in another guests room

though." There was a slight pause and Mary heard the crinkle of a plastic evidence bag. "It says: *This is just the start, you're going to pay for what you did to me.*"

There was a pause where Mary could only hear the scuffing of Corrigan's shoe on the hallway floor and the sound of the disembodied voice on the phone droning through the small speaker.

"Yes, Sir, of course, I understand. Bye, Sir,"

Mary heard the inspector swear under his breath and to her horror, walk towards the bathroom door.

She sprung away from it, turned the tap on at the sink and began splashing water with her hand in order to convey that ordinary bathroom activities were taking place. What those would be exactly from this noise she wasn't sure, but it seemed the right thing to do. The handle turned, twisted a couple of times and she heard Corrigan move away, accompanied by more swearing.

She gave it a few moments before she left the bathroom and hurried out into the hall where she was relieved to see that the Inspector had clearly gone off to find another bathroom, leaving only a single officer who watched her as she moved back towards the living room door and entered.

"Flintock," she said as soon as she had entered

and spotted him half lying on the sofa, his head back and tissue shoved up each nostril.

The officer by the door rushed around in front of her, his hands out wide.

"Now Madam, we don't want any more unpleasantness, do we?"

"Oh, I'm not going to hit him again!" Mary said testily. She looked around the room at the rest of its occupants who were staring at her slightly aghast.

"I'm not!" she protested. "Look, I just lost my temper and I wanted to say sorry."

"It's alright," Flintock said in a nasal voice. "Come on Mary, let's make it up and then maybe we can talk about your future?"

"Yes," Mary said through gritted teeth, "that would be great."

The officer shrugged and returned to his post by the doorway to the hall. Mary moved across and perched next to Flintock who struggled upright next to her.

Emily Hanchurch was glancing at her with jerky, bird-like head movements from the other end of the sofa, as Dot and Pea stared across the room with concerned expressions, clearly wondering whether they should come and join them or give her some space. She gave them a look which she hoped conveyed the latter and turned to Flintock.

"Dave, you know everything that goes on in showbiz," she said, deciding to start with some basic flattery, which she suspected would well on a someone like Flintock. "I need you to tell me everything you know about Steve Benz and Melanie," she continued, keeping her voice low so only he could hear. "What was going on between them?"

"Steve?" he said frowning. "Well, he was bloody furious with her, if that's what you mean?" He turned and looked at the figure of Emily who was facing the television again.

"I'll talk to Emily in a minute," Mary said, reading his thoughts. "But she might be a bit biased, and I want to know what really happened. Why was Steve furious with her?"

"Because of that show of his, the one that got cancelled," Flintock said, his head still tilted backwards. "It was his baby, he'd been involved in everything, even helped out with the original premise. The problem was, the whole thing had been geared around Melanie doing it. The network already had her in mind for something big and they insisted. Steve was ok with it, but then just before things were going to start actually getting into motion, she pulled out."

"She pulled out? Why? Because she was offered my role?"

"Ha! No, that was after." He looked at her with a grin. "You know how she got your job?"

"Tell me," Mary said, not sure if she wanted to hear the answer.

"She told them that if they really wanted her to take a big role, then there was one that was perfect for her, yours. She persuaded them that they could use the crack team they'd gathered for Steve's show to give *Her Law* a boost and she would be the new star, 'freshen it up a bit' was the phrase doing the rounds."

"So, she just asked for it?" Mary's eyes drifted upwards.

Had the decision really been that easy for them to make? After all the years she had put into that role, Melanie just had to ask and it was hers?"

"Melanie had a way of getting what she asked for," Flintock chuckled. "I was trying to represent her, but the truth was, she didn't really need it."

"And that's why you pestered her every bloody day about it, is it?!" Freddie Hale roared as he got up from his armchair and marched towards them.

Mary had forgotten he was even still there. With the chair facing towards the windows he hadn't been visible to them sitting on the end of the sofa.

"Now come on, Freddie," Flintock said in a weaselly voice. "I was just trying to do my best for you. The two of you working together more would have been a dream team!"

"And you didn't care what that might do to me, did you?" Freddie raged back. "You didn't care that I fell in love with her!"

Flintock's mouth opened and closed again before he looked desperately at Mary and then back to his client.

"Freddie, I didn't know. But at least you got to have the time you did with her, right? That wouldn't have happened if it wasn't for me getting you two together."

Freddie threw his glass down at Flintock's feet where, surprisingly, it didn't smash but instead bounced up onto the agent's lap.

The constable arrived at a run, but Freddie was already striding away and back out of the French doors into the grounds as he had done earlier that day, leaving the young man to look around the room awkwardly before heading back to his post at the door.

Flintock sighed and leaned back into the sofa. "If I had known he'd bloody fall in love with her, I'd have never let him near her," he muttered.

"Melanie didn't feel the same way about him,"

Mary said thoughtfully, watching the figure of Freddie Hale grow smaller as he crossed the wide lawn.

She turned back to Flintock. "And what about you? You seem to have plenty of reasons to want Melanie out of the way?"

Flintock laughed. "Course I did! That doesn't mean I was going to bump her off!"

"Not even if she was going to take your best client away from you?"

He gave a snort of derision. "Freddie wouldn't leave me, he wouldn't last five minutes representing himself like Melanie did. His looks aren't the only boyish thing about him you know, he's still got the mind of a teenager. All rushes of blood and thinking with his pants. He'll always need a proper grown up to take care of him. Anyway," he said leaning forward. "If you want someone to point the finger at, why don't you talk to your lord of the manor over there?"

He nodded towards Pea who was talking in hushed tones with Dot and glancing across at them every so often.

"Pea?" Mary said, shocked. "Why on earth would you say that?"

"Well," Flintock said, his face set into a leering grin, "last night when we were having a break from the murder mystery, I was having a wander about. I went into the library across the hall and there was Melanie and your brother kissing. She pulled away and slapped him, told him to leave her alone and marched out of there."

Mary realised her mouth was hanging open. "You can't be serious?"

"Why don't you go and ask him yourself?" Flintock grinned.

Mary got up and moved back to the other side of the room in a daze.

"Are you alright?" Dot asked as Mary took her seat at the bar again.

"Did you kiss Melanie last night?" she said, ignoring Dot and turning to Pea.

"I, well, not exactly,"

"You either did or you didn't?" Mary insisted.

"You kissed Melanie?!" Dot said, glaring at Pea herself.

"It was weird!" Pea said miserably. "She asked to see the library, so I took her in. I was just telling her about the gallery in there and she grabs me and kisses me, then straight away she shoves me back and slaps me!"

"And then what happened?" Dot asked.

"Well, then she stormed out and I realised Flintock was there, cackling away."

"Did you tell the police this?"

"No," Pea said looking down sheepishly. "I thought it might sound a bit, well, odd."

"It bloody well does sound odd!" Dot said.

Mary looked at her and noticed her cheeks were slightly flushed.

"Which way were you facing when she kissed you?" Mary asked.

"Um," Pea frowned, "I was facing the shelves and she was facing back towards the hallway."

"I'm starting to realise the kind of person that Melanie was," Mary said slowly.

"What do you mean?" Pea asked, decidedly not looking at Dot who was still sitting with a pinched mouth.

"I think she just liked to mess with people. Look at the way she was getting on everyone's nerves last night. I think she kissed you because she saw Flintock come in and thought it would be funny to make him think that you had come on to her. I think she got a kick out of it all."

She glanced past them and across to the fence windows which lead out across the grounds.

"Just take Freddie Hale for instance. Flintock got the two of them to fake their relationship, but then Freddie fell for Melanie. I think she enjoyed the power of it, that's probably why she was trying to get him to leave Flintock. Just because she could."

She looked at the two of them.

"They found a note in Steve Benz's room too."

"What?" they said in unison.

"I overheard Corrigan telling his boss about it on the phone. Apparently, it said: *This is just the start, you're going to pay for what you did to me.*"

"Blimey," Pea said, eyes wide. "And do you think Melanie sent it to him? That would definitely give him a motive."

"It would, and I'm guessing the police think so too. They've had him up in his room for quite a while now."

"Well they're still going to have to solve the problem of how anyone could have got into the room and out again with the door being locked from the inside," Dot added.

"Maybe there's some trick you can do with turning the key from the outside?" Pea said thoughtfully.

"Oh, come on, Pea," Mary said dismissively. "This isn't one of my shows where there's some tricky little move the killer made that throws everyone off."

She watched as their expressions changed to the ones of sympathy they had been wearing when looking at her for weeks.

"Oh, knock it off, you two, I can mention the show without falling to bits you know. Anyway, I doubt Steve knows how to lock a door from the outside. I doubt any of them here do."

Mary looked down as she picked at the edge of a beermat. She knew she was focusing on Melanie's killer partly to avoid thinking about the repercussions of her father's words, but it was more than that. A woman had died and no matter how horrible she was, no one deserved that.

"Someone here at the house killed Melanie, and they're trying to frame me," she said quietly. "If we're staying here tonight, I suggest we try and find out who it is."

"How on earth would we do that?" Dot said gruffly.

"We talk to people, try and find out what they were doing last night, find out if they might have wanted Melanie dead."

"I think they all might have wanted Melanie dead," Pea sighed.

"Well then, we'll have our work cut out, won't we?"

"Mary, you're not Susan Law," Dot said, raising one eyebrow.

Mary felt that bringing up the character that

neither her nor Melanie would play again was slightly below the belt but decided to ignore it.

"No, but do you think whoever killed Melanie is going to stop at just leaving a note in my room? Who knows what they have planned next? Maybe they want to bump me off too!"

Mary laughed, but then saw the serious expression of both Dot and Pea, and her smile vanished. She had said the words as a joke, but now she thought about it, it really didn't seem very funny.

"Emily thought there might have been something going on between Steve and Melanie," she said, moving the conversation on from the grim silence.

"You must be joking!" Pea said, his eyes bulging. "Steve and Melanie?!"

"I thought it was unlikely too, but he's hardly spoken since we found her and then there was all that business last night. She seemed to have a right bee in her bonnet with him as well."

"She had a bee in her bonnet with everyone," Dot said.

"And Emily said that she and Steve have been a bit of an item, but last night he chucked her out of his room and said that things had changed."

"You think something between him and Melanie had caused this mood change?"

"Could be," she shrugged.

"Well I think Flintock has got to be our prime suspect," Pea said, looking over his shoulder at the rotund manager across the room. "I mean, he had the most reason to bump her off, didn't he? She was trying to get his best client to leave him, and I wouldn't put anything past that little toad."

"Neither would I," Mary said, "and he was up at night because I saw him in the kitchen."

She frowned thoughtfully.

"I saw Freddie trying to get into Melanie's room then as well, he said she answered and told him to go away. He might not have done."

"Even if she let him in, we still have the problem of how on earth he got out and locked the door after bashing her over the head," Dot added.

"True," Mary nodded. "And in any case, I think he really loved her, he seems devastated at her death. I just can't see him doing it."

She looked up and watched Emily Hanchurch picking at her top lip as she watched the TV.

"What is it they say? 'Beware a woman scorned?' If Steve kicked Emily out of his room, she would have been out in the corridor with no one around."

She sighed and put her head in her hands. "So pretty much everyone had a motive, and everyone had a chance to have done it."

"Apart from the little fact I like to keep bringing

up," Dot said. "How on earth did anyone kill her in that room in the first place!"

Mary looked at Pea. "You don't think there are any secret passages in this old place we didn't find when we were kids do you?"

"You know there aren't," Pea said shaking his head. "We searched every inch of this place over the years. If there was anything like that, we'd know about it."

"Then we must be missing something obvious," Mary said. "I mean, killers can't walk through walls, can they? We need to start looking at other things. These notes, for example. Mine was just the bit where the killer was revealed form the murder mystery game. What time did you put the scripts in the library, Pea?"

"Oh, it was when we were all getting coats on to go up to the roof. I just threw them on the nearest table in there."

"Who would have seen you do that?"

"Well, anyone could have really. I mean we were all milling about in the hall. Flintock definitely did though. He was in the library already because he'd stormed out of the living room just before, remember?"

"I do! So, he saw exactly where you put them?"

"Of course, he was standing right by them, then I

told him to come up on the roof with the rest of us and he did."

"Ok, we know for sure that at least one person saw them there, maybe more."

"How did they get the note into your room and under the pillow?" Dot asked. I mean, they must have done it between when we all got up and when the police arrived."

"Maybe, but they could have done it afterwards. When the police first got here they were only focused on Melanie's room and everyone was wandering all over the place. Someone could have slipped into my room without much fuss."

"Wait a minute," Mary said, her mind racing. "I was assuming that the note in Steve's room was either from the real killer, trying to frame him as they did with me, or from Melanie herself."

"Yes?" Pea said slowly.

"Well think about it, why would the killer go to the trouble of ripping off a part of the script to implicate me, and then use their own handwriting on a note to Steve? I mean, it wouldn't make sense. They could just either write both notes or rip some other part of the script out that sounded like a threat or something."

"So, it's more likely that Melanie did write the note in Steve's room?"

"Exactly, which means we need to talk to him."

The door to the living room opened and Steve Benz shuffled in, his gaze fixed on the carpet.

"Well, it looks like you might have your chance," Pea said.

CHAPTER FIFTEEN

"Steve!" Emily said, rushing to him. She embraced him, her head against his chest, but Mary noticed there was a reluctant stiffness from his side, and he ended the contact swiftly.

"I need some time," he said to her quietly.

"What's going on then, Steve?" Flintock called from across the room. "Did you kill her or what?"

Steve's fists clenched by his side as his face turned crimson.

"No, I didn't bloody well kill her. Did you?"

Flintock laughed. "Course not! Anyway, I'm not the one being questioned by the police for a whole bloody hour, am I?"

Steve pushed Emily aside and marched across the room towards him but Mary jumped up and dashed across, heading him off halfway.

"Come on, Steve, just ignore him. Why don't we get some fresh air and have a talk?"

He was breathing quickly, his face straining with anger, but he nodded and turned away back towards the hallway. Mary followed him, but when Emily started along with them, she paused.

"Can I just have a word with Steve on his own, Emily?" she said softly. "Maybe I can find out why things have cooled between you?"

"Oh, OK," Emily answered in her meek, high voice.

Mary smiled at her before moving out into the hallway. She glanced to her right and saw Corrigan was standing outside the main front doors with a constable, looking out across the grounds with his back to her.

"Why don't we go up to the roof terrace?" she said, taking Steve's arm and leading him towards the staircase before he could protest.

Mary realised though that he wouldn't have protested even if she had given him the chance. His expression had returned to the glazed blankness that he seemed to have worn all morning. It was as though he had checked out of the world around him and was locked inside the one in his head.

As they walked along the corridor and passed Melanie's room she glanced in and saw two people dressed in the familiar white overalls of the crime scene profession packing away the last of their equipment. The constable who was standing at the door watched them pass through a narrowed eye but said nothing. Steve Benz, Mary noticed, kept his eyes forward.

As they stepped out onto the terrace, still littered with beakers of half-drunk mulled cider dotted around the heavy iron furniture and the plug-in cider barrel, which still on the floor with its small red light glowing on top.

"Oh blimey, we left this thing running all night!" she said, leaning over it and pulling the plug from the extension cord that was coiled next to it. Mary paused, frowning at the wound length of cable. Her hands reached out and touched the yellow dust that seemed to be all over it. She looked across the roof to the edge where the small yellow stone wall ran around the perimeter.

There was a scraping of iron on paving slab behind her and she turned to see Steve slumped in a chair, his head in his hands. She realised, with some shock, that he was crying.

"What is it, Steve?" she said, taking a seat next to him and putting her arm around his shoulders. "Was there something going on between you and Melanie?"

The thought had seemed ridiculous when Emily had said it earlier, but now, looking at the tears rolling down his slightly rounded cheeks, it didn't seem so far fetched.

"I just don't understand," he said wiping his eyes and looking up to the sky where the clouds were thickening across the darkening sky as evening approached. "How can she be dead?"

Mary resisted the urge to say, "because someone hit her over the head", at the risk of sounding callous. Instead, she plumped for, "I didn't know you knew Melanie?"

"I didn't," he said bitterly. "That's the whole bloody problem!"

"I'm sorry, you've lost me."

He took a deep breath and turned to her.

"She was my daughter."

"What?!"

"I only found out a week or so ago. I'd had a brief thing with her mother and never saw her again. I had no idea she was pregnant. Melanie pieced it together from a friend of her mother's, apparently."

"Bloody hell," Mary said breathlessly.

"I just don't know how I'm supposed to feel," Steve continued. "I know she was my daughter, but I didn't know the woman. She was angry with me, but I had no idea she had even existed! Now it's all too late. She's gone and there's no time for me to put any of it right."

"Is her mother still around?"

"No, she died a couple of years ago. I didn't really know her, just a weekend fling years ago. That's why Melanie started asking about her father." He choked back more tears. "About me."

"Does anyone else know about this?"

"No," he said, turning to her with urgency in his eyes. "And I don't want anyone to, alright?"

"Why not?"

"I just need to deal with it on my own, and I don't need bloody Flintock sneering at me anymore."

"The police though?"

"I've told them, had to. They found the note Melanie had written to me and thought she was blackmailing me or something."

"Was she?"

"No, she bloody wasn't!"

"OK, OK. I was just checking. And what about Emily?"

He shifted uncomfortably in his seat.

"Melanie didn't like her, she wanted me to stop seeing her."

Mary shook her head but said nothing. Again, Melanie messing with people's lives. What was it to her that a father she had only known about for five minutes would be seeing someone? No, she had told Steve to stop seeing Emily out of spite, and because she could. Mary wondered if Melanie had even felt any anger towards Steve for not being there when she was younger or was it all just an excuse to control people, to have the power over them she obviously craved.

"Did Freddie know?"

"I don't think so," Steve said. "To tell you the truth, I don't think she was very serious about him, she pretty much said as much to me."

He turned to her, his eyes wet with tears.

"Did Flintock kill her?"

"Why, do you think he might have done?" Mary asked.

"Oh, come on, you've met the man. I'd say he's capable of anything if there was money it for him."

"Well, I think it was someone in the house," Mary said, her face serious. "I don't think anyone could have got in through that window, and whoever it was left a note in my room."

"A note?"

"It was a piece ripped from the script of the murder mystery game. I can't imagine anyone for outside would have known to use that."

"Then it has to be Flintock," Steve said grimly.

"Or Freddie," Mary said, wanting to see his

reaction. "He was in love with Melanie, but I don't think the feeling was mutual."

Steve frowned.

"And then there's Emily," she continued.

"Emily?!" he said, jerking upright in shock. "Surely you don't think she could have had anything to do with this?!"

"She thought there was something going on between you and Melanie. She didn't know she was your daughter, she could have acted out of jealousy."

"Not Emily," Steve said firmly. "She couldn't have," he said shaking his head before sighing and rubbing his face as though trying to remove the skin. "You know Melanie got my show cancelled?"

"Yes, Flintock told me."

"She was so full of spite, so full of anger. That was my fault, my fault for not being there for her."

"You can't blame yourself, you didn't even know about her."

"That doesn't change the fact that I was her father, and I wasn't there." He jumped up suddenly. "I need to be alone for a bit, I'm going to my room."

Mary was about to protest but stopped herself. She watched him go and looked up at the wide sky overhead and followed the faint contrails of a plane high overhead, a lighter streak on the dark background of cloud. Melanie had left a trail everywhere she had gone, but hers had been one of pain and destruction.

Cancelling Steve's show, blaming him for not being there for her, taunting and bullying his new girlfriend Emily, playing with Freddie's emotions and antagonising Flintock. What had it all been for? Where had it got her? Her head bashed in on the floor of a musty old bedroom.

She got up, stretched, and walked over to the small wall that ran along the front of the house, being careful not to lean on the crumbling yellow stone as Dot had done. She looked down across the grounds to her right where the lake wallowed at the bottom of the slope, its waters an oily green. Her ran along its shore to the folly and she frowned, the words of her father's message to Pea running through her mind.

You'll find answers under a fool's bottom

CHAPTER SIXTEEN

S he turned and hurried back across the roof to the doorway that led into the house. She bounded down the spiral staircase as she had done so many times as a child and stepped out onto the landing where movement up ahead made her slow. She watched the constable she had seen earlier leading the two crime scene operatives down the large staircase. She slowed as she reached the door to Melanie's room and glanced through the narrow gap where it hung open.

There was no one there.

Without thinking, she stepped inside and pulled the door half closed again behind her. She stepped forward and then froze as she saw the dark stain of blood in the middle of the floor. She was suddenly glad of not having had anything to eat yet today, or she might well have had to see it again.

She tore her gaze away from the stain and looked around the room. There was a sideboard with a mirror and chair, a double bed and bedside tables. None of the furniture seemed likely to have been the cause of the head injury, and Corrigan had said the crime scene team had ruled it out in any case.

She noticed a suitcase in the corner of the room, its lid lay open and she could see several dresses folded neatly inside. Melanie had come prepared.

She went into the bathroom and poked around but found nothing other than a few beauty products laid out by the sink. Her heart fell a little at the comparison to the huge range of products she used in the daily battle against her own aging skin. All Melanie had done was thrown some eye shadow and lipstick on and she had looked fantastic. Mary had to trowel on creams and potions these days, just to be able to pass for forty-five.

She stepped back out into the bedroom feeling disappointed. There seemed to be nothing else to discover from the room. She had no idea what she had expected, but it was more than this. Of course, it was silly to think that the police would have overlooked anything that she could spot, but, still, she had wanted it to happen.

She stepped to the still open window and looked down the sheer wall to the grass below. She was still sure that no one could have climbed up to it. She began to pull her head back into the room when she noticed the outside windowsill had a fine layer of yellow dust across it.

"This is still a crime scene, Miss Blake," Corrigan's voice came from behind her. She jumped as she spun around.

"Bloody hell! You frightened the life out of me!"

"I think that's what happens when you get caught sneaking around in a room where a murder has been committed," the inspector answered.

"I was just having a quick look, to see if I could see anything odd."

"You mean something we missed?"

Mary felt her cheeks reddening. "Well, I don't know how efficient the Tanbury police are, deal with many murders, do you?"

"More than you'd think," Corrigan replied sighing. "We cover the whole north of Addervale and you'd be surprised how many of these quaint little villages have their secrets."

Mary again thought of her father and his strange words to Pea. Yes, she was well aware that people had secrets.

"Well, I'll just leave you to it," she said, moving

towards the door. He reached out and gently put his hand on her arm. She stopped stiffly, as though someone had passed an electric current through her.

"Have you found anything more that you'd like to tell me about your fellow guests?" he asked.

"No, nothing important," she answered, trying to ignore how close he suddenly seemed to be to her and how it was making her pulse quicken.

"I'd rather you told me everything and let me be the judge of what's important and what isn't," he answered. "Has anyone threatened you?"

"No," Mary answered, slightly taken back by the question.

"This isn't a game, Miss Blake, someone is trying to frame you for murder, and I don't know what their next move might be. Be careful."

"Thank you," Mary said pulling her arm away, "but I'm quite capable of looking after myself."

She left the room without looking back and moved quickly towards the staircase. Why was this man getting under her skin so much?

She looked down into the hall as she descended and breathed a sigh of relief when she saw it was empty. She didn't want anyone to follow her, not even Pea. She'd feel like an idiot if she were wrong.

As she reached the front door it opened in front

of her to reveal the rounded figure of Hetty Wainthropp.

"Hetty!"

"Mary dear! Are you OK?!" the little woman shrieked, dropping her basket and grabbing Mary in a tight hug.

"I'm fine," she answered, trying to breathe. "So, they finally let you in?"

"Yes, bloody nightmare it is out there. As soon as those press people realised I knew you and Percy, they wouldn't leave me alone! Asking me all sorts of questions they were, but I didn't tell them nothing," she finished proudly, grinning as she picked up her basket again. "I've brought all sorts to cook up, I'll get going right away."

"Great, thank you, Hetty,"

The small woman nodded and moved off towards the kitchen at the back of the hallway and paused. "I don't believe what they're saying about you, Mary, don't you worry about that."

"Oh," Mary said, unsure of what else to say, "thank you." She knew the press would be hot on the idea that she was responsible for Melanie's death, but worrying about it wouldn't help.

She stepped out into the grounds and was relieved to see that Corrigan was no longer around.

She moved quickly to the right and began heading across the wide expanse of grass towards the folly.

How had she not thought of it as soon as Pea had mentioned it? How had he not realised? It was so obvious! But she wanted to be sure, she had to go and look for herself. She reached the small stone building and stepped inside.

The word "folly" means foolishness, and follies were built in country houses around England as a whimsical, indulgent act of the upper classes for centuries. "Under a fool's bottom" had to mean under the stone bench that ran along the back wall.

She got down on her knees and peered underneath the space, her hand reaching out and feeling along the large, solid slabs of stone that formed the floor.

There was nothing there but the rough grooves between the stones, no gap, and no secret panel. She was about to give up when a crack in the wall made her pause.

She reached out and pushed her fingers into the gap and felt the stone to the left of the crack move. She dug her fingers in further and the stone slid out onto the floor.

She pulled her phone from her pocket and turned on the torch function, shining its white light into the hole that now appeared under the bench. At the back was a small piece of faded paper. She felt her pulse race as she reached in and pulled the scrap from its hiding place.

"Mary Blake?" a voice came from behind. She spun around, holding the note behind her back in her right hand.

A man was standing before her, his hand stretched out in front of him holding a small, silver Dictaphone.

"Do you have any comment on the fact that you are the number one suspect in the murder of Melanie Shaw?"

"No, I bloody don't!" Mary said, standing upright quickly and advancing on the man.

He was a young, scrawny-looking man with an eager face that gazed at her expectantly.

Mary glanced at the Dictaphone and decided against saying anything further. Instead, she attempted to move past him. He moved to let her pass but went the same way as Mary and they collided. Instinctively she held her hands up in front of her and the scrap of paper fluttered to the ground on impact.

He reacted first, bending quickly and picking it up before she had recovered her balance. She watched his eyes scan the sheet quickly before handing it back to her.

"I'm so sorry," he said putting the Dictaphone away.

Over his shoulder, Mary saw two police constables running towards them across the grass.

"Not as sorry as you're going to be when those police officers get here," she said smoothly.

He turned, saw them and laughed.

"I look forward to seeing you again Miss Blake!" he called as he turned and ran off along the shore of the lake, the officers veering to run after him.

Mary turned away from them and headed back to the hall, clutching the scrap of paper tightly in her hand as she waited for her heart to stop thumping as though it would burst from her chest.

She entered the hall to find Corrigan standing towards the back wall by the entrance to the kitchen. Ignoring him, she hurried towards the stairs and ran up them. She didn't want to read whatever was on this paper in front of anybody, not even Pea. She would show him later.

She continued making her way upwards until she found herself on the roof terrace where, for a moment, she looked up at the now ink black sky, taking deep breaths of the cool air as she tried to compose herself.

Mary walked to the seating area and perched on the edge of a hard iron chair before looking down at the note she had had squeezed into her fist.

It was handwritten, and she recognised her mother's writing at once, causing a lump of emotion to rise in her throat.

For the sake of the family, our baby
    we hide,
And though she is gone, you will find
    her inside
One day, time will come to bring her
    back home
And in order to do so, you will need
    a tome
And although this book is no longer a
    tree,
Still but for woods, her you can't see
In Crickwood you'll find, by a
    babbling brook,
Using your glasses, in 100 look.

MARY LET OUT a long breath she hadn't realised she had been holding.

...*Our baby we hide*...

So, she did have another sibling, one that her father had hidden from her and Pea.

She frowned as she read through the words again. Why would her father write this cryptic message and hide it in a secret location? Surely it couldn't be the location of the child. He or she would be forty years old now and could be anywhere in the world. So, why keep this hidden all those years and tell Pea to uncover it now?

There was a crunch of gravel behind her and she half turned as something heavy hit her across the head and the world turned black.

CHAPTER SEVENTEEN

"You'll be fine, but you'll need to rest for the rest of the day," the doctor said sternly. "No television, no reading, and I don't want you to sleep for a good few hours."

"Right," Mary croaked. She had been lucky enough not to require the services of many doctors over the years, but this one had the bedside manner of a hippo and the physical presence to match.

"And try to be more careful in future," the woman said as she rose and turned towards the door.

"More careful?!" Mary said to Dot when she had gone. "I was hit over the bloody head! What does she expect me to do? Wear a crash helmet?!"

"How're you feeling?" Dot asked, peering at the back of Mary's head.

"Oh, I'm fine, I would just like somebody to tell me what the hell is going on!"

Mary had opened her eyes from her prone position on the roof to find Inspector Corrigan standing over her. Confused and woozy, she allowed herself to be checked over firstly by a constable with first aid training, and then latterly by a doctor in her bedroom. Nobody had answered her questions about who had hit her. In fact, everyone had been particularly evasive, and she had noticed a number of whispered conversations, both when she was being helped down the spiral staircase from the roof and also as the doctor had checked her over.

"Something's happened, Mary," Dot said, her square face set

"Well, of course, something's bloody happened!" Mary said, "someone whacked me over the head!"

"No, something else. It's Flintock, he's dead."

Mary's mouth fell open and stayed there as she tried to read her friends face to see if she was joking.

"Flintock's dead?!"

Dot's lips pursed in silence for a moment before she answered.

"He fell from the roof,"

"The roof? You mean... while I was up there?"

"It looks like that, yes."

"So, whoever hit me over the head pushed him off!"

"Maybe, or he did it himself."

Mary pushed herself up from the beaded swung her legs over the edge.

"What do you mean?"

"The police found a note in his pocket apparently, it says he killed Melanie."

"Bloody hell," Mary said breathlessly, "he hit me over the head so that I didn't stop him?"

"That's what the police think, but I don't know why he wouldn't just wait until you'd gone away."

"Well, bearing in mind he killed someone and then threw himself off of a building, I'd say he wasn't thinking straight, wouldn't you?"

"Oh, right. Of course," Dot answered, but with the air of someone who had not been in her right mind and couldn't imagine what that would look like.

In this case, Mary thought she might have a point.

"I have to say, I can't quite imagine Flintock feeling remorse over anything," she said slowly. "And the idea of him killing himself just seems, odd. I mean, I don't think I've ever known someone who loves himself as much as that man." She trailed off as something occurred to her.

"What if someone pushed him off?"

Dot frowned at her, her lips pursed. "You mean, the same person who killed Melanie?"

"Yes! What better way to get the attention away from them than to blame it on someone else?"

"An interesting theory," a voice came from the bedroom door. They looked up as Corrigan pushed the door open from where the doctor had left it ajar.

"There are some things that don't make sense about all of this, though," he continued as he moved into the room, closing the door behind him. "Let's assume that Miss Blake here is not the killer for a moment, shall we?"

"Yes, let's assume that," Mary answered testily.

"Then we know that the killer of Melanie Shaw tried to frame you by leaving the section of the murder mystery script."

"Which doesn't make any sense," Mary said. "I mean, who did they want us to think put it there? Melanie could hardly have done it after I'd bashed her over the head could she?" She caught the expression of them both. "Theoretically, obviously," she added quickly. "My point is that if someone knew I had killed her and then put the note there, why wouldn't they tell the police?"

"Maybe they were blackmailing you with the information?" Corrigan said flatly.

Mary stared at him.

"You mean someone like Flintock? Who I then threw off the roof and faked a bang on the head?"

"The thought had occurred to me," he said. "But as we're assuming you are not the killer in this scenario, let's think of why someone else might have left that note even though it didn't make sense."

"They must have panicked," Mary shrugged.

"Exactly," Corrigan said smiling. "It's the action of someone who isn't thinking straight, someone who's desperate and is acting without thinking."

"Someone who's desperate enough to throw themselves off of a building," Mary added.

"Maybe," Corrigan said. "But why now? This person's first thought was to point the blame at somebody else, to deflect attention away from themselves at all costs. Now, a few hours later and they are suddenly so full of remorse they want to end it all? No. I think those few hours gave this person time to think. They thought of a better way to frame somebody."

"To kill Flintock and leave a note on him saying he did it?"

"Exactly," Corrigan said, pulling an evidence bag from inside of his jacket pocket. "Have a look at the note."

Mary took the bag and peered through the plastic

to the paper inside. There was a single line, written in blue ink:

I killed her, time to pay

"You can barely read it," Mary said, passing the note to Dot who studied it as she had done. "He must have been shaking like a leaf when he wrote it," Mary continued.

"Either that or someone was deliberately trying to hide their own handwriting when they wrote this," Corrigan said taking the note and placing it back in his inside pocket.

"You mean like that old trick of writing it with your left hand?" Mary asked.

Corrigan raised an eyebrow. "Could be. In any case, our list of suspects has grown smaller. I'm afraid I'm going to have to confine you all to your rooms from early evening. We'll have men on every door and more at various points around the house." He looked at his watch. "It's gone two already and I know that no one has had anything to eat yet, so I think it best you all get something. I know that a woman, who insisted I called her Hetty, by the way, has been cooking up a storm down there, half my men are drooling at the smell. Shall I get your brother to send some up to you?"

Mary's heart gave a jolt as she thought of Pea and the box she had found.

"When you found me, did you find anything else?"

"Ah, yes. I wondered whether you were going to bring that up," Corrigan said, his eyes twinkling suddenly in the dim light of the room. "Very mysterious."

"You read it?" Mary asked, aghast.

"Of course I did. This is a murder enquiry. Can you tell me what relevance it has to the case?"

"None whatsoever."

"Ok then, can you tell me where it came from and why you had it?"

Mary sighed and glanced at Dot who was sitting, tight-lipped with a look of utter confusion on her face.

He's right, this is a murder enquiry, Mary thought. There's no sense in trying to hide anything.

"I found it in a secret panel under the stone seat in the folly down by the lake."

"What on earth?!" Dot said, her eyes widening.

"I went there because my father had told my brother there was something there relating to our family."

"And how does that scrap of paper and its

contents relate to your family?" Corrigan asked, his eyes narrow and serious now.

"I'm not quite sure," she paused and looked up at him. "You've read it, it's just some silly game my mother cooked up, she was always one for crosswords and cryptic clues. It has sentimental value though, and so I would like it back."

Corrigan seemed to think for a moment before giving a small nod and heading for the door. "We'll have to keep it, for now. I'm afraid it is evidence until proven otherwise, but we'll get it back to you as soon as we can. Please make sure you both get something to eat, won't you?"

"What on earth was all that about?" Dot asked once the door had closed.

"Go and get Pea and some food and then come back up here and I'll tell you all about it."

Dot gave her a stern look, sighed and left the room on her errand.

Mary lay back on the bed and stared up at the ceiling. Flintock was dead. She could hardly believe it. She reached her hand up to the patch of gauze that the doctor had applied to the wound on her head and sighed.

CHAPTER EIGHTEEN

"Are you sure you're remembering that right?" Pea said, frowning.

"Of course I'm not remembering it right!" Mary exclaimed rolling her eyes. Her brother questioning her being high up on her list of annoyances. "I only read it once and then I was clubbed over the head! All I know is they said they had hidden their baby and then there was something about Crickwood."

Despite having eaten, Hetty had apparently whipped up a round of bacon sandwiches for everyone in the house including the police, the dull ache from her head was still making her grouchy.

"And the inspector has it now?"

"Yes, they picked it up when they found me. What do you think it means?"

"Well, I remember Crickwood. Do you?"

"I know where it is, if that's what you mean?"

"No, I mean that we used to go there quite a bit in summer, but it was before mum died. I think she might have had some distant family there at some point. It's only about fifteen miles away."

"And they hid a baby there?! What on earth does that mean? You don't think one of them had an affair, do you?!"

"Wait a minute!" Pea said, his face splitting into a wide grin. "Do you know, I don't think they did!" He laughed.

"What is it?" Mary said glancing at Dot who looked equally baffled.

"Don't you remember? All those stories dad used to tell us about Grandpappy treasure hunting?"

"Treasure hunting?" Dot exclaimed.

"Oh, it wasn't treasure hunting," Mary said dismissively, "he was just a hoarder. Travelled the world and grabbed every little thing he could find and brought it back here. You should see the attic and cellar, it's full of the stuff."

"Yes, but I'm talking about his baby!" Pea cried laughing again and throwing his hands up in the air with excitement.

Mary frowned. "What do you mean 'Grandpappy's baby'?" she paused, light dawning from a distant memory that fought to the surface.

"You don't mean that nonsense about the Russian egg?!"

"Yes!" Pea cried. "Didn't dad always say it was true?"

"Well yes, but he used to tell me I was descended from a fairy princess, so I think we should take the children's stories with a pinch of salt, don't you?"

"Would someone mind telling me what's going on?" Dot said folding her arms, her beady eyes flicking back and forth between the two of them.

"When we were little," Pea began, "our dad used to tell us this story about our grandfather. In his younger days, between the world wars, he was quite the party animal. He spent his days in the clubs and cocktail bars of London, playing cards, gambling and chasing the opposite sex."

"I always wondered where you got it from," Dot interjected, looking pointedly at Mary.

"Very funny," Mary replied in a voice dripping with sarcasm.

"Anyway," Pea continued, "one night he was making his way back to the apartment he used when he was in town and he saw a man being attacked in the street by three others. Grandpappy had fought in and survived World War One and was as tough as old boots. He knocked two of the attackers clean out and the third ran away.

He knelt beside the man who had been attacked and asked him if he'd been robbed. This poor chap was in a pretty bad way, but he could talk. He said "No! They attacked me because I am a foreigner! Not for my bag, the fools! Now, you must take it, it will be no good to me where I'm going. Do more than me with it, save it for your family, and look after it like a baby."

Pea, getting carried away with the part had spoken these words in a distinct accent.

"Was this man German, then?" Dot asked, causing Mary to burst into laughter.

"No, he bloody wasn't!" Pea said, looking hurt that anyone could confuse his attempt at a Russian accent. "Anyway, the man died, but Grandpappy took the bag he had had with him and inside it, was a decorative egg worth millions."

Pea rattled out this last sentence like a machine gun and folded his arms.

"Millions?!" Dot said in a breathless voice.

"Oh, come on Dot, it's nonsense!" Mary laughed. She turned to her brother and saw his glazed expression.

"What if it isn't?" he said in a whispered, faraway voice. "What if it really was the answer to all our problems?"

"You can't be serious?!" Mary gawped at him, incredulous.

"Think about it, Mary, why else would dad hide a note in a secret panel in the folly?!"

Mary opened her mouth to reply, but the words escaped her as she considered her brother's point. Why would her father have gone to all that trouble?

Donald Blake had been a good father to both her and her brother. He had told them stories, played with them and been there when they needed it. Despite this, he had been a straight-laced, sensible man much of the time and wasn't prone to flights of fancy and imagination. The idea of him creating an elaborate treasure-hunt-style clue hidden within the grounds that he had told no one about until now when his mental functions were diminishing, seemed ridiculous.

"Wait," Mary said, "maybe someone else did know?"

"What do you mean?" Pea asked.

"I mean that in the note, dad said '*we* hid our baby', he must have been talking about mum."

"Well, there you go!" Pea said, "You can't tell me that they both would have been in on hiding this note if it was just a joke or something. It must lead to something, and maybe it's the egg!"

"Well we're not going to find out unless we can

get that note back, and that's not going to happen until this case is solved."

"I thought it was solved?" Pea said, with a puzzled expression.

Mary filled him in on the recent developments before the three of them fell into a thoughtful silence, which was broken after a few moments by Dot.

"Did you see some reporter when you were out in the grounds?"

"Oh, yes I did. I was in the folly getting the box out and some weedy little man sprung up behind me. I think the police kicked him out again. How did you know?"

"When I was fetching Pea I saw the TV reporting that you had been acting 'suspiciously', as though you were trying to bury something and that the police had been informed."

"Oh, bloody hell!" Mary said throwing herself back onto the bed. "I've had enough of all this!"

"I'm sure Inspector Corrigan will work out what's going on soon," Dot said in the calm voice of someone who believes in authority absolutely.

"He hasn't got a clue!" Mary said sitting up again. "The only person who could have had any reason to kill Melanie, other than me that is, just fell off the roof. And we don't think he did it, even though he confessed through a note! I just can't see..." she stopped suddenly, her train of thought derailed by a sudden landslide of previously unseen possibilities.

"Oh, blimey," she said in a whisper.

"What is it?" Dot asked, looking at Pea as though she suspected the blow to the head might have made some more lasting damage than previously thought.

"Come on," Mary said jumping up. "We need to go and check some things!"

CHAPTER NINETEEN

"Slow down!" Dot called from behind as Mary rushed along the landing and leaned over the bannister to see Inspector Corrigan talking to two officers.

"Inspector!" she called out as she headed down the stairs towards him.

He gave a final word to the officers who left through the front door and moved towards the staircase, reaching it as Mary descended the last step.

His arm snapped out, steadying her as she stumbled to her left.

"Sorry," she said shaking her head to clear it, "I think I got up too early. I need to know if you think you could get a fingerprint off rough stone," she said in a rush.

"Off rough stone? It would be difficult. What do you know, Miss Blake?"

"Damn. What about a wire?"

"If it has a plastic coating, possibly."

"Right." She pushed past him and headed for the door, leaving Dot and Pea, who had followed her down the stairs, to give the inspector sheepish grins as they passed.

Mary jogged down the steps and turned left, striding with her long legs as she headed around the house.

"Mary!" Pea called out from behind her, "Where on earth are you going?!"

"I'm going to count windows!" she said triumphantly.

"She's gone loopy," Pea said quietly to Dot as they hurried behind her.

"It's the blow on the head," Dot replied. "I knew I didn't like the look of that doctor, I don't think she knew what she was doing at all. All that nonsense about not reading."

Mary stopped and turned back towards the house and looked up at her bedroom window.

"What are you looking at?" Pea asked as they reached her.

The three of them stared upwards in silence.

"I'm counting windows," Mary said quietly after a moment. "Think about how someone might have killed Melanie in that room," she said turning to them.

"We already have thought about it!" Pea cried. "It's not bloody possible!"

"It must have been possible, Pea, because the woman is dead, isn't she?"

"Well, yes, but how?!"

"I can't see anyone being able to get through that door," Dot said thoughtfully. "So, I guess you're thinking it was the window, Mary?"

"I am! Actually, you're the perfect person to ask this Dot. Look up at the house and point to, no. Wait. You've been in my room. I need to get the others to look at it."

"Mary, for goodness sake!" Pea cried again, waving his long arms in the air. "What on earth are you talking about?!"

"Think about the guests who haven't been in my room or yours," Mary said excitedly. She was feeling a rush of adrenaline she hadn't felt in years. Not since the early days of shooting *Her Law* when the world had seemed a more exciting place when she had felt more alive.

"OK, I'm thinking about them," Pea said folding his arms. "But what's that got to do with anything?"

"If you asked them to point out Melanie's room, which window do you think they'd point to?"

The three of them looked up at the house again.

"Well, that one!" Pea said exasperatedly. He pointed a long finger towards the third window in from the left.

"No," Dot said in a quiet but firm voice.

"They'd think about how many doors were in the corridor and then they'd think about the one window in their room."

"Exactly!" Mary put her hands on Dot's shoulders from behind and squeezed them. "So, which window would they think was hers if they didn't know my room had two in it?"

"Bloody hell," Pea said in a whisper.

"They'd think it was the second window," Dot answered. "Which is in your room."

"So that means if the killer did use the window to kill Melanie, they might have thought it was the next room along, and who was in that?"

"Flintock!" Pea cried turning back to her, his face alive with excitement.

"Who died just a few hours later," Mary said smugly, placing her hands on her hips. "Maybe the killer decided to finish the job they had wanted to do in the first place and thought they could wrap Melanie's murder up at the same time?"

"Bloody hell, Mary," Pea said, looking at her in awe. "You're a genius! It's like you're actually Susan Law!"

"Hold on," Dot said in the tone of someone who was generally against any inflating of Mary's ego, which she already considered to be of more than sufficient size. "I thought we'd agreed that it would be pretty impossible for anyone to climb up there?"

Mary sighed and looked up at the sheer wall again.

"Yes."

She walked over to it and ran her hand along the unforgiving stone.

"It's still a bloody good idea though," Pea said encouragingly. "You should tell the inspector."

Mary pictured Corrigan and wondered how he would he would react to her theory. He would listen, she thought. He was the kind of person who looked into your eyes and listened to every word you had to say, soaking your thoughts up like a sponge. You had to watch yourself around someone like that. Oh, everybody says they want someone who really listens to them, but when faced with the reality of talking to someone who would remember every word you say in the heat of the moment, they'd soon regret it.

She imagined him listening and then nodding, thanking her for the idea and telling her that he would consider it. She couldn't think of anything worse. She liked to know where she was with people. Tell her it was nonsense or tell her it was brilliant. Don't keep your cards close to your chest, don't hedge your bets.

She realised she had been going over the conversation with Corrigan in her head for at least a minute, with the other two shuffling in silence behind her, she stared at the base of the wall.

Why did he seem to infect her brain like this? On a day when she had discovered a dead body, been knocked unconscious and then discovered that someone else might have been killed as she lay there, he seemed to bother her almost as much as these events.

"Come on," she said turning away from the wall. "Let's go back inside."

CHAPTER TWENTY

S teve Benz and Emily Hanchurch were sitting at the small bar in the living room in silence. They both looked up as Mary and the others entered but said nothing.

Hetty was on the far side of the large room, apparently talking to an armchair.

"And I thought you were ever so good in that," Hetty was saying in her loud, yet lyrical country voice. "And it was such a shame that they had you get trampled on by that horse," She looked up and noticed Mary, Dot and Pea.

"Oh hello!" she said, bustling over. "Now Mary, let me have a good look at it," she reached up to Mary's head where she stared at the bandage the doctor had applied as though she could see through it. "What you need is a good rest and a gin and tonic," she said in a matter of fact voice as she led Mary to the sofa before hurrying off towards the bar.

"Can you make that three?" Pea called after her, causing her to turn around and give him a look that implied she would, but he was pushing it.

"What about Steve Benz," Mary said with a whisper as she looked across to the bar.

"What about him?" Dot asked.

"Well he had just found out that Melanie was his daughter, maybe he didn't like how Flintock was speaking to her?"

"It's a bit of a weak reason to try and murder someone though, isn't it?" Pea replied. "I mean, I doubt he's even had time to come to terms with Melanie being his daughter. It seems a bit of a leap from there to killing some man because he was a bit rude to her."

Mary sighed, he was right.

"In any case," Pea continued, "if your theory is right, Mary, and Melanie was killed by someone getting through the window somehow, wouldn't they have known it wasn't her as soon as they got in there? And wouldn't she have screamed or something?"

"Maybe they didn't get in the window. Maybe they fired something through it? It was open after all. Then they might not have known who they were firing at in the dark."

"But it would have been dark outside, and light inside," Dot said thoughtfully. "Whoever was in there would have been lit up. You'd have seen whoever you were aiming at."

"Well, aren't you two a great bloody help?" Mary huffed as Hetty returned with a tray of four drinks.

"It's not five o'clock here yet, but I'm sure it is somewhere in the world," she said as she handed out the tall glasses.

Mary looked out of the long French windows at the fading light. It would be night soon. The prospect of spending the evening in Blancham Hall suddenly didn't seem so appealing to her. Her childhood home had been turned into a place of death.

"What's going to happen to this place, Pea?" she asked.

Her brother sighed and swirled the ice in his glass.

"I think we'll have to sell up. I've been approached by a conservation group, they would like to restore it and open the grounds to the public."

"Oh," Mary said, unsure of what to feel.

"What would you think of that?" Pea asked. "This place is yours too."

"No it isn't, Pea," she said smiling at him. "You were the only one of us who ever fitted here, you know that. This was somewhere I stayed when I was younger, it wasn't home like it was for you." She laughed suddenly, "I was the black sheep of the family."

"Do you know?" Pea said, looking up at the ornate ceiling. "After all the paperwork and endless bills, and things falling apart all over the place, I think the only thing I'll really miss is the fishing."

Hetty laughed as Mary and Dot grinned.

"You always were one for your sports," Hetty chuckled. "Even though you were bloody useless at all of them!"

This time Mary laughed too. The combination of a gin and tonic and her friends around her lightened her mood considerably.

Pea had always loved fishing, heading off from a young age down to the lake where he would sit for hours without so much as a nibble.

Fishing.

Something was gnawing at the back of Mary's mind, like a worm that had discovered a juicy apple, but found its skin a tough barrier.

"Fishing," she said out loud, for no apparent reason that either she or anyone else could be sure of.

"You ok there, Mary?" Hetty said, looking at her oddly.

"Yes," Mary answered slowly. "I think I am."

She straightened up, drained the rest of her gin and tonic and turned to her brother.

"Pea, do you have a football here at all?" She raised one eyebrow. Since they had been children, Pea had loved the game. Unfortunately, with his slender build and the coordination of a baby deer on ice, he never actually played, other than to constantly walk everywhere with a football either under his arm or at his feet for months, until the next sport came along.

"Yes," he said, his cheeks glowing somewhat as he glanced at Dot's inquisitive expression. "There's one in my bedroom if you must know."

"And have you got another long extension cord like the one you used on the roof for the mulled cider?"

"Um, yes, I think there's another one in the storage cupboard on the roof. Why?"

"Don't worry about that, I just want you to get the football, give it to me, and then take Inspector Corrigan and all go and stand in Melanie's room, OK?"

She watched her three friends look at each other, reading the concern on their faces.

"My head is fine!" she said rolling her eyes. "Come on!"

CHAPTER TWENTY-ONE

M ary rummaged around in the small wooden box that acted as a cupboard for the various items that were used on the roof terrace from time to time. A small barbecue was positioned in one corner with logs for the fire pit piled between its legs. There were wires and extension leads and space where the mulled cider vat normally was. Mary grabbed a long white extension cord from the top shelf and moved across the roof as she unwound it.

Would this work? She didn't have a clue, but in the absence of any other theory, it was worth a shot. She cursed herself for not thinking of it sooner. The noises she had heard in the night, the open window, where Melanie had been in the room. It all made sense now, but only if this experiment worked.

She peered over the edge of the wall and looked

down at the windows below, being careful not to lean on the crumbling wall where she could see that a large chunk had already tumbled down into the grass.

She gently lowered the end with the plug down over the wall and fed out the wire.

"You are clever Mary, I'll give you that,"

She spun around towards the voice. Freddie Hale was leaning against the wall of where the staircase rose onto the roof via the door. He had a smile on his lips, but there was no humour there. His eyes were sunken and red, his cheeks pale.

Mary left the wire hanging over the edge and moved away from the wall, moving sideways further into the middle of the roof.

"Freddie, is everything OK?" she said, trying to keep her voice light.

"No, Mary, nothing's OK. I'm not sure it ever will be now." His voice was flat, unemotional. He began to move towards her and her heart began to pound.

"It was an accident, wasn't it, Freddie?" she said, "You didn't mean to hurt Melanie, did you?"

"No, but I meant to hurt someone."

"Flintock? But why?"

"He wouldn't let me leave him," he took another step forward. "Melanie had said she couldn't respect someone who wouldn't stand up for themselves. She said I had to leave him or we were through."

"But Flintock wouldn't let you go?"

Freddie shook his head and took another step forward. She could see now that his eyes were wet with tears.

"He had me tied up in a contract that was unbreakable. I signed it years ago when I was younger. I didn't have a clue what it all meant then, but it would have bankrupted me if I'd left."

"So, you decided to just remove the problem?"

"I was drunk, I wasn't thinking straight!" he snapped suddenly, his hands reaching up and wrenching at his mop of hair as his face twisted in anguish.

"I just couldn't let him ruin everything!" he moaned, his fingers clawing his cheeks, leaving red, angry marks. "He just wouldn't let me breathe! I'd met him downstairs in the kitchen, he was laughing at me. He told me that I shouldn't have been naive enough to sign something I didn't understand. He said we were locked together and that he wasn't going to let Melanie get in our way. I came up here and finished the cider."

"When did you realise it wasn't Flintock you'd killed?"

He recoiled as though she had slapped him.

"I didn't know, I couldn't see, it was dark." He spoke in short bursts, as though the words were coming out as unwillingly as vomit. "I tried to get her to let me in, I was going to tell her what I'd done."

"That's when I saw you on the landing, knocking at her door?"

"Yes. She didn't answer," his voice faded away, his eyes glazed.

Mary inched to her left, eyeing the doorway that led to the spiral staircase downwards. As she was judging the distance and whether she would be able to past Freddie before he reacted, the door opened and Steve Benz stepped out, followed by Emily Hanchurch.

They froze as they surveyed the scene. Mary's eyes flickered to Freddie who still seemed locked in his own, dark thoughts.

"And once you realised you had killed her, you decided to finish the job you had wanted to do on Flintock?" Mary said in a voice loud enough to carry to the two newcomers.

Freddie looked up at her with lifeless eyes.

"It was his fault. She died because of him. He had to pay."

Mary listened to the flat, staccato speech as her eyes flickered to Steve who was standing behind him. He had gestured to Emily to stay and picked up a short length of wood that had been leaning against the wall to the right of the doorway.

Mary realised she had given Steve away as Freddie's face creased into a frown of confusion and he began to turn.

She acted on instinct. The frustrations and stress of the last few weeks pouring out of her in one pure moment of rage and anguish. She charged at him, hitting him in the back with her shoulder as hard as she could, and sending them both sprawling onto the gravelled surface.

Freddie was fighting to right himself from the moment he hit the floor and threw Mary off to one side just as Steve Benz swung the length of wood, bringing it down on Freddie's head with a dull thunk that rendered him motionless on the floor.

"Thank you," Mary said breathlessly as she pulled herself to her feet. Steve was standing over Freddie with fire in his eyes and a furious expression that Mary had never seen in him before. It contorted his plain face into something to be feared.

She watched as he slowly raised the wood once more as he loomed over the prone figure. With horror, Mary realised that Steve Benz was going to strike Freddie again, and then again and that he wouldn't stop until the man that had killed the daughter he had just met, had shared her fate.

She tried to shout, but her throat had tightened in fear. Instead, it was Emily who shouted.

"Steve!"

Steve Benz froze his arms high above his head, the wood still. Mary watched the fury fall from his face, to be replaced by sadness. His arms sagged and the wood clattered to the floor. Emily put her hand around him and turned him away from them.

The door leading down to the house banged open and Mary looked up to see Corrigan framed in the doorway. His deep brown eyes scanned the scene in an instant before he headed towards Mary at speed.

"Are you ok, Miss Blake?"

"I'm fine, I'm fine," Mary said getting up and brushing herself down. "Though you might want a constable to come and arrest Freddie Hale for the murder of both Melanie Shaw and Dave Flintock." She put her hands on her hips feeling every bit the character of Susan Law that she had played for so many years.

Corrigan smiled and turned to the uniformed officer who had followed him onto the roof.

"Check Mr Hale's injuries and if he's ok, make sure he's restrained," he said in a jovial tone. "Well, Miss Blake," he said turning back to her. "It seems you keep turning up in the middle of this mess. Now you're telling me that you've discovered who the culprit is, and it's Mr Hale here?"

"She's right," Steve Benz said, stepping towards them with Emily on his arm. He was composed again now; all traces of the furious anger Mary had seen earlier were gone. "I heard Hale admit it. He was going to kill Mary too until I hit him over the head."

"Ha!" Mary exclaimed. "He could have tried, I'm the one who tackled him to the floor."

Freddie Hale groaned himself awake as he was raised to his feet by the constable.

"We'll need to take a statement from all of you, and I think it's time we ran the gauntlet of the press and got you all down to the station. First, though, I believe you were going to show us something that would shed light on how Melanie was killed inside a locked room?"

CHAPTER TWENTY-TWO

"It was the windows that got me thinking," Mary said when she and Corrigan were alone on the roof in the fading daylight. The others had all been sent down into Melanie's room again, still with no idea what they were doing there.

"So, you're going to show me how someone could have got in and out of that window? And they did it somehow from up here?" he said, peering over the edge of the short wall.

"No. The first thing to think about is which window was he aiming at?"

"OK," Corrigan said slowly, fixing her with an attentive gaze.

"Freddie was drunk, he was angry. He wanted to get Flintock out of his life and clear the path for him and Melanie. My guess is he looked over here and thought back to when Dot knocked part of the wall over earlier in the day. The whole thing is crumbling to bits."

Mary placed her hands on her hips, a pose she had used in the show many times when she was about to reveal the killer. She had to admit, she was enjoying herself. She was exhausted, her head hurt and she wanted nothing more to be curled up in front of a fire with a G and T in her hand, but right now she felt more alive than she had done in months. Maybe years.

"So, he thought back to the corridor downstairs. He knew Flintock's was the third door along, so naturally, he counted three windows along too."

Corrigan smiled, nodding. "But your room has two windows, so the one he was actually focused on wasn't the third bedroom along, it was only the second, Melanie Shaw's room."

"Exactly," Mary said, picking up the electrical cable she had taken earlier from the cupboard and feeding it over the edge of the wall as she had done before.

"What he needed to do next," she continued, "was to get Flintock to open the window." She peered over the edge and Corrigan copied her. As the plug, dangling at the end of the wire, reached just above the window, she lifted the football Pea had given her.

"If you heard this tapping on your window, where would you assume it came from, bearing in mind you were on the first floor?"

"I guess I'd think someone was throwing stones up from the ground," Corrigan answered.

"Exactly, let's see, shall we?"

She lowered the plug until it tapped on the glass pane of the window. She felt a chill as the noise she had heard in the night came back to her.

They heard the catch of the window being opened and she pulled up the plug a few feet and readied herself with the football. Her brother's head appeared through the opening and scanned around the grass below. At once, Mary threw the ball downwards. And watched as hit Pea on the back of his head, making him shout out in shock.

"Sorry, Pea!" she called down, laughing.

Pea vanished back into the room cursing.

"So, he got her to look out of the window and then dropped something heavy down?" Corrigan said breathlessly.

"A piece of the wall, can you see a large chunk missing just down there?" She pointed a few feet to their right where a clear gap was visible. "Can you remember this morning when I stubbed my toe on something? It was a piece of this wall. I'm guessing it might be the piece that Freddie used to try and kill Flintock."

"But ended up killing Melanie instead," Corrigan finished.

"He didn't realise he had. All he saw was a figure in the dark. I saw him the next morning, he was devastated, but it was more than that, now I think about it. He was horrified as well. He couldn't deal with what he'd done and he blamed it all on Flintock."

"So, he decided to kill him and frame him for Melanie's murder."

Mary nodded. "He'd already failed with his clumsy attempt at framing me. He obviously wasn't thinking straight and just panicked. He knew I had been the murderer in the game, so he just tore that part off and snuck it in my room."

"It all makes sense, but we'll need proof."

"This wire is a spare, the one that was out on the roof is over there and hasn't been touched by anyone else as far as I know. I noticed it had some yellow dust on it earlier which must have come from sliding it over the crumbling wall. You might get some fingerprints from it. In any case, I'm not sure he'll have much fight in him now. I think the fact that he killed Melanie is only just really hitting him."

"You know?" Corrigan said, smiling at her in that easy, relaxed way which seemed to be his default setting. "You're quite impressive, Mary Blake. Not many people could have been present at the scene of two murders, which they then become the prime suspect of, and not only handle it, but solve the whole thing."

Mary felt herself blush at the compliment. What was the matter with her? She wasn't the type to blush from the attention of a man, she was usually the one making the man blush.

"Don't worry," she said with a hint of mischievousness, "I won't tell your superiors that I had to help you."

He laughed. "Thank you, I think I'm going to have enough trouble working out what to say to the press."

"I hope you caught that one who broke into the grounds earlier."

Corrigan's face clouded over.

"No, we didn't. He shot back over a wall before my lot could catch up to him. I asked around, no media outlet seems to know who he was from the description, but of course, they wouldn't admit if it was one of theirs anyway."

Mary frowned. Something was niggling at the

back of her mind again, something she couldn't quite place, but that she didn't like.

"Can I have the note of my father's that I found?"

He paused for a moment before answering. "You can, I can't see it has any relevance to any of this. Do you want to tell me what it's all really about?"

"I told you, just some silly game of my father's."

"So why is it I don't believe a word you are saying?"

"Because I'm not that good an actress," Mary said smiling. "I need the note tonight, I need to take it somewhere tomorrow."

He sighed. "Very well, but can I ask something of you?"

"What is it?"

"When you're ready, can you take me for a drink and tell me what it was really about?"

"Maybe," she smiled back. "But only if you promise not to suspect me of murder again."

"Deal."

They smiled at each other under the dark blanket of the night that had fallen almost unnoticed around them.

CHAPTER TWENTY-THREE

"**A**nd they just offered it to you? Just like that, the day after Melanie died?"

"Yes," replied Mary. "Apparently all this publicity will really liven the show up and they think I'm the right person again to take it on."

"And what did you say?" Pea continued as he leaned forward from the back seat of the car that Dot was guiding through the narrow country lanes.

"I told them I wasn't interested."

"Except I heard there was quite a lot more swearing than that," Dot said with a hint of a smile.

"I bet!" Pea laughed. "What are you going to do next?"

Mary looked out of the window and took a deep breath.

"I don't want to act any more."

"Oh, right. What do you want to do?"

"I wondered if you could use some help on the estate? I could move back for a while?"

Pea turned to her, his narrow face split into a broad smile.

"Mary, I'd love it!" Then the smile faltered. "Though I don't know how long we'll be able to stay."

There was a long silence as Pea focused on the road and Mary stole glances at his concerned face.

"I could sell my apartment," she said. I mean it's mortgaged to the hilt, but it would give me something.

"No," Pea said firmly. "You shouldn't have to do that. Your whole life is in London, you can't give it all up to try and keep some crumbling pile from falling into ruin."

"Then what are you going to do?"

"Well, first, I'm going to spend a few days with my little sister and the wonderful Dot in an old place from our childhood, chasing some mad clue that our dad appears to have left. I think that's enough for now. Let's let the real world of bills and responsibilities go to hell for a while, shall we?"

"Sounds bloody marvellous," Mary laughed. She looked down at the piece of paper in her hand and re-read the clue. She knew this was all a wild goose chase, but Pea was right, right now she didn't care.

They rode over the crest of hill and a wide, rolling valley appeared before them.

"Well, it's still as beautiful as it always was," Pea said.

"I still don't remember it," Mary frowned.

"I bet you do when we get into the town," Pea said as he slowed the car.

"Bloody hell," Dot grumbled. As they had descended, the road had narrowed until the wing mirrors of the car were scraping against the grass and brambles on either side. A white car had appeared further down the hill and was heading towards them, apparently unconcerned at their approach in the narrow lane.

"Pull in here," Mary said, pointing to a gate set back from the road. Pea turned the car towards it and they bounced as they moved over the deep tractor tracks that led into the field beyond.

The car slowed as it aimed to navigate what was still a tight squeeze. Mary watched the boxy vehicle until her eyes fell on the face at the window.

It was young man with a narrow, angular face. She straightened up quickly and leaned forward as the car pulled alongside.

"Don't worry," Pea said. "There's room to get through"

"It's not that, it's that man!"

As the car crept past them, the gaze of the three friends focused on the man. He turned towards them as he passed alongside and Mary gasped.

"That's the reporter who broke into the grounds! The one who found me pulling the note from the wall!"

"Well, that's a bit of a coincidence," Pea said, steering the car back out not the road.

"Yes," Mary said grimly. "A bit too much of one bearing in. Mind he had a look at the note."

"He saw the note?!" Pea said, incredulous.

"Yes! We bumped into each other and I dropped it for a moment, he read it before he gave it back to me."

"Blimey," Pea said, slumping back in his seat.

They road the rest of the way down into the small town of Crickwood in silence. Each of them wondering if the reporter had already found the answers the note alluded to.

CHAPTER TWENTY-FOUR

A few minutes later, the three of them were walking out onto the main street of Crickwood, which stretched out before them like a postcard.

A shallow river dominated the town, running alongside the main road and crisscrossed with stone bridges that led to a network of smaller streets on the other side. Sunlight glinted off the water and the small cafes and tourist shops that lined this side of the street only contained a few people in this, the off-season.

"So, where are we going to start?" Dot asked as they surveyed the beautiful scene in front of them.

"Well the obvious place to start is the river," Pea said. "I mean, I know it says a babbling brook, but that's got to mean the river surely?"

"I don't know," Dot answered. "It also mentions trees, doesn't it? It could be out of town in the countryside somewhere."

"Honestly," Mary sighed and shook her head at them. "You two are useless, aren't you? You're missing the main point, it said we're looking for a book."

"You could still hide a book in the countryside," Dot grumbled.

"Yes, but then it says," Mary pulled the note from her pocket and read from it, *"And although this book is no longer a tree, still but for woods, her you can't see"*

She looked at their blank expressions and rolled her eyes. "It's talking about the saying, *you can't see the wood for the trees.* So, something is hidden amongst a lot of other things the same, and where do you find a lot of books?"

"A library?" Dot chipped in.

"Finally!" Mary said, pointing to a small, square building with four round pillars forming a porch outside the front entrance, "Come on!"

Mary was unable to keep the smile from her face as they walked along the river path towards the library. She had been quite pleased when early this morning, while showering the remaining exhaustion from her tired and aching body, she had realised this part of the clue. She still had no idea what the final line meant, *Using your glasses, in* 100 *look* still had no meaning to her, but she was feeling confident. She had just solved a murder after all, and the whole country was talking about her as some kind of crime-fighting genius. Of course, she hadn't been overly pleased at being dubbed "Mary Marple", she wasn't that old.

It had been a late night and a morning of police statements and dealing with the press, who had relentless. Not only had the murder of a famous actress and a publicity agent stoked the fires of publicity, but someone had spoken to Hetty, who had proceeded to portray Mary as a modern-day Sherlock Holmes.

The press, when unable to contact Mary herself, contacted her agent. Terry had seized the opportunity and had quickly built Mary up to be the police forces secret weapon. Excited at the opportunities, Terry had been ringing Mary's mobile so often that Pea had shown her how to temporarily block his number.

It was a small wonder that they had managed to give the world the slip for this short trip to Crickwood, but they had managed it by using a small gate at the estate that led down a footpath to the village. There, Hetty had arranged for someone to deliver a hire car. Mary had had no doubt that the two young people who had dropped it off and returned in their own vehicle would inform the press almost immediately, but it had given them enough time to get away.

The library building of Crickwood was positioned next to the river and shared the rather tatty building that housed it with the town hall and museum. The four stone pillars that marked the entrance were overkill on a building of this size but leant it grandeur at least.

They entered and followed the signs into the left-hand side of the building where a young woman in a bright yellow blouse buttoned up to her neck smiled at them.

"Good morning," she said in a sweet, singsong voice before looking back to the computer in front of her.

"Excuse me," Mary said, "We're looking for something, but we don't quite know what it is,"

The woman looked up again, her eyes widened and her mouth formed a small "O".

"You're Mary Blake!"

"Yes," Mary said smiling. "Look, I know it's a strange thing to ask, but I think there's a book in this library that I need to look at, but I'm not sure of the title."

"Oh, don't worry! It happens more than you think! What sort of thing were you after? Something on crime, I bet? I think we've got something on the investigation side of things that would be just the ticket!" She moved out from behind the counter and began heading towards the stacks.

"No, it's not that kind of book," Mary said, stopping her in her tracks and cursing Hetty for telling the world that she was a budding real-life detective. "Well, at least, I don't think it is. All we've got is this line that goes 'Using your glasses, in 100 look'. Would that mean anything to you?"

The young woman grinned, looking between the three of them with a playful expression.

"Is this some kind of set-up? Wait!" she said with a sharp intake of breath, her hand moving to her chest. "Am I on TV?! Is this some kind of hidden joke show?! Is that what you're doing now?"

Mary looked at Dot and Pea, who matched her expression which suggested this young woman might well be a few sandwiches short of a picnic.

"I'm sorry," Mary said in what she hoped was a reassuring tone. "I'm not quite sure what you mean?"

"Well, I'm not dim!" She laughed. "James has just been here looking for that same book, and..." she paused, the smile vanishing from her face. "Oh, no!

I've made a right fool out of myself, haven't I? So, he was part of it?"

"This James, was he a young, keen chap? High cheekbones?"

"You do know him!"

"We've met," Mary said, turning to the others and saying in a low voice "The reporter we passed on the road."

"How do you know he was looking for the same book we are?" she continued to the librarian.

"Well it's the same clue, isn't it?" The woman said, looking more confused than ever. "'Using your glasses, in 100 look', it means the *Glass Centurion*."

"What the hell is the *Glass Centurion*?!" Mary said loudly, throwing her arms in the air.

"The name of the book James needed!" The young woman returned looking utterly bewildered.

Mary realised she was upset and took a deep breath.

"Can you show us the book?"

The woman nodded. "I've only just put it back," she said, turning towards the rows of shelves. "It's over here. He tried to take it out but he didn't have a library card. I told him he could sign up for one, but he was all funny about giving me his ID and said he'd just look at it here."

She led them through two aisles as she talked

before she stopped and pulled a large hardback book from the shelf.

"I looked the book up after he'd left as I'd never heard of it and, it's funny, this book was actually donated by someone called Blake."

Mary had just felt as though someone had sucked the air from her at the mention of her family name.

She took the book that was offered to her and flicked through the pages. It appeared to be the fictional story of a Roman soldier and looked nothing out of the ordinary. She flicked to page one hundred, thinking that the 'centurion' theme might continue further than just the book title. There was nothing there.

"Did this James find anything in this book, do you know?"

"He was definitely looking for something," she answered. "Which I thought was a bit odd as it's not a reference book or anything, it's a story."

"Did he say anything to you while he was here? Anything at all about the book?"

"Actually, he did ask me something quite odd. He wanted to know how a pair of glasses could mean a particular page in a book. Very strange."

"I take it you couldn't think of anything?"

"Well, I said that a number eight on its side looks a bit like a pair of glasses, that's all I could think of."

The young woman shrugged. "Look," she said, planting her hands on her hips, "What is all this about?"

Mary ignored her and instead flicked to page eight of the book, Dot and Pea peering over her shoulders. There in the margin were two words, written in her mother's hand.

Sookie's grave, like the fool

"Ha ha!" Pea shouted jumping backwards and clapping his hands together.

Mary slapped the book shut.

"Did this James ask you anything about Sookie's Grave?" she asked the librarian.

"What? The one in the churchyard? No, he didn't mention it. Why?"

"You are a credit to the library service!" She beamed at the young woman as she handed her back the book, "if this works out, I'll buy you the mother of all rounds at the local pub tonight!"

She turned and headed for the door with a Dot and Pea trailing after her.

"What on earth is going on?!" Dot said once they reached the crisp air outside.

"That reporter's got it wrong!" Pea laughed, "he must have!"

"Probably thinks it's some family member or pet that died and he's gone back to Blancham to find out," Mary smiled. "It's funny, I couldn't remember this place for the life of me, but I remember Sookie's grave."

"Will one of you please tell me what's going on here!" Dot moaned, hurrying to keep up with the long stride of the two Blake children who were moving across one of the small bridges which crisscrossed the river towards a churchyard that was set back from the road a short distance away.

"You'll see," Mary said, not slowing her pace.

They reached the churchyard and moved along its flagstone path until they reached a small gravel path which jutted out to the right. Mary and Pea followed it without hesitating. It led through the churchyard towards the back wall where a large grave loomed. It was a tall cross, the top of which had been fashioned into the large head of a cat that grinned widely. Below it across the arms of the cross was the word, *Sookie*. At its base were a few bunches of flowers and even a child's drawing of a black cat.

"Sookie was the town cat a couple of hundred years ago," Mary said to Dot as they stopped. "There are all sorts of myths and legends about the animal, that she was a witch's cat, or that she was a woman cursed to be a cat by a witch, all sorts. No one really knows why she was so loved, but they built her this big gravestone and buried her along with the humans of the town. It's become a bit of a tourist attraction now and people think that if you leave her some flowers or a drawing it's lucky," She gestured at the offerings which lay at the foot of the grave.

"But that reporter wouldn't have known about it?" Dot asked.

"Not likely, it's not very well publicised. It's more of a local thing, but we came here so much we knew about it and came all the time. It's just a good thing he didn't ask that woman at the library and assumed it was something to do with us back at Blancham."

"Wait a minute," said Pea, "I seem to remember that dad paid for renovations on this place one year. Paid for the path to it and for the gravestone to be cleaned up etc. Maybe they had something added then? I can't see anything though," he said, looking around the area.

"What did the note in the book say, though?" Mary said as she moved across to the old stone wall that ran along the edge of the graveyard. "*Like the fool* it said. Just like the first clue was hidden in stone after being described as under a fools bottom..." she bent down and examined the wall. Studying the large stones that ran along its base. Her fingers found the edges of one that seemed different to the others, the gap around it being larger and deeper than the surrounding ones. She dug her fingers in and slowly wiggled the stone left and right until it came out of the wall, the accumulated mulch of the years tumbling from it as she did so. She reached into the hole and pulled out a square wooden box, rising as she dusted it off.

"Bloody hell," Pea said, his voice hoarse. "You don't think it's really the egg, do you?"

"Only one way to find out," Mary said, lifting the metal clasp which hung over one side of the lid. She lifted it back to reveal a velvet lined cushion, set into the middle of which was a small, silver egg encrusted with diamonds.

The three of them stared at it in silence for what seemed like hours.

"I think I'm going to need to break that day time drinking rule again, Dot," Mary said quietly.

"Me bloody too," Dot replied. "Me bloody too."

Get FREE SHORT STORY *A Rather Inconvenient Corpse* by signing up to the mailing list at agbarnett.com

READ on to see the first chapter of the next in series!

MORE FROM A.G. BARNETT

Brock & Poole Mysteries

An Occupied Grave

A Staged Death

When The Party Died

Murder in a Watched Room

The Mary Blake Mysteries

An Invitation to Murder

A Death at Dinner

Lightning Strikes Twice

A DEATH AT DINNER

Mary, Dot, and Pea were slumped on the wooden bench in the echoing corridor as they stared off into space with unseeing eyes. Mary's throat felt dry. If she could have spoken a word, she would have asked in a firm voice for a gin and tonic. Instead, she unfolded the small sheet of paper the auctioneer's assistant had handed her and stared at the number. There were a lot of zeros.

They had been ushered into a corridor at the back of the auction room, away from the baying press who had been stalking them since the discovery that had led them here.

"Did that just really happen?" Pea said from her right.

"It did," Dot replied from her left.

"Bloody hell," Pea added.

"That about sums it up." Mary nodded, finally finding her voice.

There was another period of silence until Mary stood up and rammed the piece of paper into the inside pocket of her tan leather jacket. "Right, I think it's high time we all went to the nearest pub to drink gin and tonic until all of this makes some sense."

There were dazed murmurs of agreement as the others rose from their seats and the three of them moved along the corridor towards the discreet rear entrance that an employee of the auction house had assured them would provide an escape from the press pack.

"Mary! Mary Blake!"

She turned to see a round, tubby man waddling down the corridor towards them.

"Mary, how do you feel about the record sale of the Fabergé egg you recently discovered?"

Mary frowned at him, wondering how the reporter had evaded security to find his way back here.

"Do you know?" she said, folding her arms. "I have absolutely no idea, but I'm sure I'll work it out in time."

The man stopped, frowning in confusion, as a security guard appeared behind him at a run and steered him back towards the public area with a firm clasp of his arm. Mary turned away and pushed open the doors before stepping into the bright sunlight.

"They will not leave you alone after this you know," Pea said, sighing as he followed her out and they headed down the road.

"Oh, they'll get bored, eventually. Now I'm not on TV, I'm nowhere near as much of a pull for them. This will do," she said, pointing down the street to a ramshackle pub.

Inside, the light was appropriately gloomy for a central London pub that had probably been serving pints to the city's citizens for hundreds of years. Mary and Dot took up residence at a well-worn and sticky table in the corner while Pea gathered them all gin and tonics at the bar.

"Well at least this means you've got the money to keep me employed," Dot said as she pulled a tissue and wiped the portion of the table in front of her.

"Quite the opposite," Mary said with a glint in her eye. "I need not work at all anymore, a personal assistant seems rather pointless, don't you think?"

"I think we both know that you don't pay me to help you professionally, you need me to make sure you can get through any twenty-four-hour period without descending into chaos."

"Point well made, if a little harshly," Mary answered as Pea arrived and placed their drinks before them. He sat heavily onto a battered wooden chair and sighed, his cheeks were flushed as red as his hair from the excitement and adrenaline of the auction, he looked tired.

The three of them seemed to have been at the centre of a whirlwind since they had discovered a Fabergé egg thought to have been lost for over a hundred years. Mary and Pea's grandfather had been entrusted the egg by a Russian man whose identity was unknown, their parents had later hidden it in the wall of a village graveyard. Now, brought back into the world from its hiding place by Mary, her brother Pea and her friend Dot, it had been identified as the Alexander III commemorative Fabergé egg, thought lost in the tumultuous fall of the Romanov's as Russia's ruling family. It had sold for twenty-one million dollars, and now they had to decide what they would do with it, and the rest of their lives.

"So what about you big brother?" Mary said, turning to him. "You don't have to worry about keeping the estate above water at least, but what next for it?"

"I don't want to run it at all anymore."

Mary blinked in surprise. "The estate?"

Pea looked up at her. "Of course, the estate! I'm finally free of it!"

"But I thought you enjoyed it?!"

"Oh, really Mary," Dot said with a tut and shake of her head. "For someone who professes to be such a people person, you do miss what's right under your nose sometimes."

Mary's gaze switched between her friend and her brother in confusion, causing Dot to roll her eyes.

"Mary," Pea said leaning forward, "I never wanted to run the estate, it was always dad's thing, not mine."

"Then why on earth did you do it?!"

Pea laughed. "Oh come on! You know it would have broken dad if I hadn't taken it on. It was all he ever wanted. He wanted the family to stay at Blancham forever, and that would only happen if we could somehow make the estate self-sustaining."

"And now you have the money..." Mary said, thinking the implications of this through.

"... I can hire a full-time estate manager," Pea continued, "and finally do something I want to do."

As he spoke, his eyes glazed over, his voice trailing off.

"So what's that going to be?" Dot asked.

"I have absolutely no idea," he said in a hollow voice.

"Well, that makes two of us," Mary said, lifting her glass to clink against his.

"Three actually," Dot said, raising hers.

"Do you know?" Mary said after a moment of silence, "There's a saying that I think is appropriate right about now." They both looked up at her expectantly. "They say that money can't buy you happiness, but I'd like to test the theory."

The others laughed and suddenly the tension of the morning cleared as though a storm had released an oppressive humidity.

Mary's phone buzzed in her jeans' pocket. She pulled it out and glanced at the number calling, unrecognised.

"Hello?" she said, placing the device to her ear.

"Mary? It's Spencer, Spencer Harley."

Her brow wrinkled as she tried to place the name. "Spencer Harley?" she said, looking at Pea carefully to gauge his reaction.

"Spencer from that holiday in France?" Pea said in a whisper, "With mum and dad?"

"Yes," Spencer continued, "I know it's been a while, but I wondered if I could invite you down to my neck of the woods for the weekend?"

"Oh, right," Mary said, unsure of what to say.

"There's a restaurant down here that's having an anniversary bash and thought you might want to join us?"

"Right, well that sounds nice, but..."

"I've seen you in the papers recently and I think it would be of some interest to you..."

Mary paused. She had been in the papers recently. Being credited with catching the murderer of a young actress who was your arch-rival, tended to do that. Especially when soon after you discover a missing treasure of the art world.

"Could you just hold on a moment?" she said before covering the mouthpiece.

"It's Spencer Harley, he wants me to go to some restaurant bash this weekend, something to do with me being in the paper."

"Say yes," Dot said immediately. They both turned to her. "We've all just being saying that we need to figure out what we do next," she said, "maybe we don't need to figure it out, maybe we just need to go with the flow and see where it takes us. Ask if we can all come, I could do with a nice meal."

Mary's mouth fell open at this unusually carefree attitude of her oldest friend, but she didn't have time to be suspicious, Spencer was still on the phone.

"Yes Spencer, that would be lovely," she answered, eyeing Dot carefully. "Would it be ok if my brother and friend came along as well?"

"Of course! The more the merrier! Let me give you the details."

Printed in Great Britain
by Amazon

56550758R00158